THE

MELODY

THE
MELODY

JIM
CRACE

HAMISH HAMILTON
an imprint of Penguin Canada, a division of
Penguin Random House Canada Limited

Canada • USA • UK • Ireland • Australia • New Zealand • India • South Africa • China

First published in Great Britain in 2018 by Picador, an imprint of Pan Macmillan, London
Published in Hamish Hamilton paperback by Penguin Canada, 2018
Simultaneously published in the United States by Nan A. Talese/Doubleday, a division of
Penguin Random House LLC, New York

www.penguinrandomhouse.ca

*Publisher's note: This book is a work of fiction. Names, characters, places and incidents either
are the product of the author's imagination or are used fictitiously, and any resemblance to actual
persons living or dead, events, or locales is entirely coincidental.*

LIBRARY AND ARCHIVES CANADA CATALOGUING IN PUBLICATION

Crace, Jim, author
      The melody / Jim Crace.

Issued in print and electronic formats.
ISBN 978-0-7352-3521-2 (softcover).—ISBN 978-0-7352-3522-9 (electronic)

      I. Title.

PR6053.R22M45 2018   823'.914   C2017-907163-7
                                            C2017-907164-5

Book design by Maria Carella
Cover design by Andrew Roberts
Cover image: zakaz86/Getty Images

Printed and bound in the United States of America

10 9 8 7 6 5 4 3 2 1

Penguin
Random House
HAMISH HAMILTON CANADA

. . . but we are by now weary of the piety of galleries and the gaudiness of churches. Instead, we stroll along the Avenue of Fame, where, among the busts and bronzes of little distinction, we find the life-sized statue of a naked boy, placed there through the benefaction of a will in 1939. Our guide assures us that the boy steps down from his pedestal at night and causes trouble in the town. He has witnessed it himself, he says: the trouble and the pedestal, though not the child.

—ALAIN TANCRED,
One Hundred Towns of Character and Charm
(revised edition, 1952), translated by the author

PART ONE

MENDICANT GARDENS

1

IT WAS NOT UNUSUAL for Alfred Busi—*Mister Al*—to wake up in the shallows of the night and overhear a cacophony of animals, hunting for food in his and his neighbors' metal rubbish bins or drinking water from the open drain, water that the residents had used to clean their teeth or wash their clothes and dishes. When he was a married man, he tells me, such shadowy disorders were not at all disquieting. He only had to press his nose again into the warm cloth of the woman in his bed and there could be a pair of Minotaurs at his bins for all he cared. For thirty years and more, he'd found full comfort with Alicia, with *Missus Al*, his wife, and wanted little else. But in the loveless, fallow times that came with widowhood and age, he was reduced to sleeping on his own and so he could be troubled by the bins and drains, or at least detained by them from rest. And then he would slip out of bed, go tiptoes on his naked feet to peer out of the high window that looked into the yard and, westward, into town. In the two years since Alicia's death, he'd seen—and made a list of them in the daybook on his desk—a bestiary of dogs and cats, a monkey once, the usual deer, the usual swarms, a feral pig, a bird too black and indistinct to be named with any certainty, reptiles, pigeons, rodents of a dozen kinds—not only rats, though there were tumbling multitudes of rats—and, naturally, the poor. If he was wasteful, throwing out some cuts and slices still good enough to eat himself, then he was wasteful for the poor.

That May night when Busi suffered the cuts and bruises on his throat and face—we've seen the photograph—had been a soggy one, with a careless wind intent on keeping everyone awake. He might not have slept much anyway. He'd drunk a little more than usual, three or four sweet tots of Boulevard Liqueur, a woman's drink, Alicia's, and so, encouraged by the anxieties of the coming day, a headache was inevitable. He had agreed to wear his medals and his suit and make a public speech. The prospect was alarming, even for a man who in his time had sung in the greatest halls and auditoriums and, on one occasion, years ago, not far from here, to almost everybody living in our town. His show was tannoyed from the stage into the streets, a "modest gift for the needy and the ticketless," he'd said, hoping that the modesty would attach to him as well as to the gift.

Busi did not try to fool himself where music was concerned. He knew his singing voice of late had lost some of its caverns and its peaks. Age had weakened and reduced it, as it must. But what he missed in range, he'd gained in craft: the trick of knowing how to make the most of his shortcomings, how to employ the latest microphone for volume and dimension, how to waltz and shimmy with its rigid stand, how to murmur like a lover or a confidant rather than resound mightily as he could when young, "the barrel-chested maestro of acoustics," "the market crier of the song," a human megaphone. So, even at the age of sixty-something, he was hardly anxious about performing. Besides, the venues where he still gave occasional recitals of his cele-

brated, proven repertoire to his loyal fans and whatever strays
could be delayed by his voice were more likely to be small foy-
ers or bars close to home than great, capacious halls abroad. He
didn't care—he welcomed it, in fact—that sometimes his only
payment nowadays would be applause. He had some savings
from his most successful years and he owned his family house.
In his widowhood, his affection for the building was all the love
that he possessed. Not selling it, not "milking the market," as he
was urged to, bullied to, more frequently these days, was a regu-
lar if modest satisfaction.

The offers from housing factors, architects, and agents—
none of whom had any desire to live in the villa and enjoy it, but
only plans to knock it down and build—were delivered to the
door in stiffly embossed envelopes, but mostly left unread. Busi
knew that was not shrewd financially but it was wise in every
other way. Being devoted to the place where you live and pro-
tecting it, he could easily persuade himself, was not proprieto-
rial, little more than title and mastery over an assembly of walls
and ceilings. No, rooms could be comforting companions, especially if they had been hung and furnished by your wife. The
styles and choices were all hers. She was indented in the cushions and the chairs; the mirrors had grown old and silvered in
her company; that curlicue of ring marks on the tabletop was
where she'd left her cup a thousand times; those antique crystal
glasses had tipped toward her lips; that bedspread was the one
that covered her the day she passed away. Death does not tidy
up or sweep as it departs. We all of us leave traces other than the
ashes and the bones. Her ashes, actually, were still at home, in
their brass and rosewood presentation coffer on the piano top;
she rattled slightly with *fortissimo*. She should be scattered in a

peaceful place, but her husband could not bear her parting from him entirely.

Their home—one of the two surviving seaside villas at the old end of the promenade, beyond the new hotels and restaurants and the fashionable marble-faced apartment crescents with their costly slivers of an ocean view—had been a passion for them both. The grand—the *grandiose*—first-floor window with its curving wrought-iron balcony and flaking paint afforded three contrasting and distinctive outlooks that added value to what had become in recent years, since Alicia, a run-down property. To the west, there was a narrow prospect of the town—the seaside shopping street, some modern frontages, its ramshackle aquarium and a skyline rising steeply from the bay, which was a largely unspoiled frieze of historic towers, domes, and spires. To the east, there were glimpses from the balcony of wooded slopes and the progress-defying remnant forest beyond, the only daytime darkness that we had near town, the almost-wilderness, a confined headland of trees hemmed in between the buildings and the sea cliffs. This was what the French would call *garrigue* but we born here know better as the *bosk,* a tangled, aromatic, salt-resistant maze of sea thorn, carob, and pine scrub. And to the front? A paved square where cars and carriages could turn, and a fussy planted garden with benches from which passersby could watch the blinding cinema of sea.

This was where, on Sunday afternoons and summer evenings, the more cautious citizens in their buffed shoes would end their walks along the waterfront and head back into town on paving slabs rather than chance their ankles on the pebble beach or risk the unattended forest tracks. The older ones would look up at the house, perhaps, knowing that their *Mister Al* had lived there all his life. Was that the man himself, standing at the window, with a novel in his hand? Was that him, old and naked from the waist up, balanced on a chair to change a bulb? Was that the singer eating lunch, alone, on his defiant balcony? Then, afterward, they might even catch themselves humming "Babel, Babel" or "The Drowning Sailor Speaks of Love." Those were the titles that still earned Busi modest royalties and kept his reputation—unlike the hero of his song—just afloat, its head above the water.

Yes, Busi was a moderately prosperous man, prosperous in everything except love, let's say. There might no longer be a pressing need for him to sing for supper but he had been a lifelong devotee of making music, and so perform he would, he hoped, until at least the hour of his death. He'd join in the hymns and liturgy at his own funeral, he liked to tell an audience. They'd press their ears against the coffin lid and catch his lasting voice or hear him singing from his little urn of ashes. That would be his one reward, and theirs. Yes, *Mister Al* would hold us rapt right to the end. No one who knew him doubted that. He never doubted it himself. Nonetheless, presenting a formal address while wearing a tie and without a piano at his side, as he had undertaken to do at noon, would be an ordeal. What he called his "missing limb" would be on show for everyone to see; he had never had the gift of making people laugh, the power to amuse, except in song. And so the very thought of standing up to speak and not to sing laced his stomach stiff and tight as boots. Busi badly needed six or seven hours of unbroken sleep if he were to face the day ahead with any confidence.

But on that night before the speech, the animal banquet in the yard had been uncommonly disturbing. Usually these nocturnal looters went first for water at the drain and then took what they could, the easy pickings, the offcuts and the peel and anything that could be gripped and dragged through the bins' air vents and punctures. Then they'd hurry off elsewhere and Busi would be left in peace, resting if not quite asleep. This time, though, the wind had helped the larger feeders, strengthened and emboldened by their hunger, to topple the bins and let them spill. The containers had been full and ready for emptying, and so there was enough to keep the feeders busy in the yard and keep the neighborhood awake for quite a while.

Busi peered down from the bedroom window for a second time that night. The clouds had curtained out the moon and stars. The only illumination, from the streetlamps on the promenade at the front of the house, was too low and distant to trespass in the yard. He turned an ear toward the four glass panes. There was always more to hear than see in these unlit hours—not only the animals but also the buffeting of the wind, the swish and crackle of the trees, the clonk of loosened gates, and, farther off, the sea.

Feeders at the bins would normally follow the trampled game trails in the bosk and come down the loose limestone escarpment at the back of the Busi villa. Busi hadn't scrambled up it since he was a boy, but he could remember coming home more than once with thorn-shredded legs, a twisted ankle, and bruised hands, to be greeted by the zesty sting of salve as his mother wiped him clean. The bosk behind his home and to its east was treacherous and steep, so any creature descending to the yard and breaking cover there was bound to signal its approach with shifting lime scree or the dislodging of a rock or the snapping of a branch, and Busi could then expect on busy nights a tinny symphony of bins and the bickers, the barks and snarls of warring animals.

There were the usual noises, certainly. And movement too. Now that his eyes had adapted to the gloom, Busi could make out the liquid shadows of his visitors and the eye shine of cats, but little else. When Alicia was still alive, he'd occasionally seen torch lights in the yard and then had known that there were humans at the feast, some street folk hoping for a rich man's meal, some beggars from the Mendicant Gardens who'd come into the yard to push their old boots through the scrap and spot whatever might be edible, or usable, or valuable, or bright. The poor were quieter than the other animals, and warier. They were both predator and prey, and understood what trespassing amounted to, if caught. They'd lift the lids and turn the bins as carefully as maids unpacking porcelain. Only once had one of them attempted to come into the villa, but he—or she, perhaps—had taken fright as soon as he had sensed the pair of faces looking down from the high window. Busi and Alicia had been woken by the forcing open of the yard gate—not a maneuver yet perfected by any animal—and now could witness their visitor's alarm and his retreat, and hear the hurried and receding footsteps on the street.

On this night, as far as Busi could tell, the diners were too small and confident and raucous for beggars. He knew that there would be no point in banging his knuckles on a windowpane in the hope of scattering these guests. At best, some moist and apprehensive faces (if animals have faces, that's to say) would look up idly at the noise and then continue snouting. Mostly he would be ignored. He hardly merited the baring of a fang. The ill-tempered rap of old man's bone on glass was not a language they could bother with. Feeding counted more than fear.

"Get yourself a shotgun," his nephew had advised, too frequently; his nephew, Joseph, on his dead wife's side and a man not miserly about sharing his opinions. "Sell up, Uncle," he would say. "This place is far too large for one." Or "Why not take in summer lodgers? Unless you *want* your rooms to stale." Or "You ought to find yourself an honest maid." Joseph had no idea how his uncle hoped to pass his days, and wanted none. Shotguns suited him, so shotguns should suit everyone. But, as Busi liked to tell his friends and any fans or journalists who visited the house, he was—at least, since he'd discovered microphones—one of nature's doves. Alicia had often called him that—the Chanson Dove, the singer with the Feathered Voice (both titles used for concert tours and his recordings). He was a *coo*-ner rather than a crooner, she had said, too often in his view; a lyricist of his finesse could not approve of feeble puns no matter who the composer might be, no matter that she was adored. He was "the broker of tranquillity," according to the obituary already waiting to be printed on his death. His low notes were "his sedatives, and his aphrodisiacs." His reputation—his self-image, actually; his vanity—rested on his seeming calm and his composure. His worth was proven by his modesty. Busi could hardly be the man, no matter how disturbed he was, to open out the high window and point a weapon into the night, let alone disturb his neighbors' sleep with gunshot, let alone harm anything.

There was a gentler weapon, though, behind his bedroom door: not quite a cudgel but stouter than a walking stick, a weapon that had only once drawn blood. Boy's blood, to be exact. He reached for it before he went out onto the landing. He knew full well there'd be no sleep for him unless he made the effort straightaway to, first, urinate—dilute that evening's alcohol with water from the bathroom tap—then find the pillbox for some painkillers to chase off the worsening headache, and then go downstairs, undo the bolted doors, and venture into the yard himself to pull the bins back on their feet. He'd have to see if he could find something heavy or some rope to secure their lids.

The stick, he persuaded himself, was only for any dogs that might be in the yard. A cornered dog, unlike a monkey or a cat, would rather bite an unarmed man than back away from feeding. But all dogs, even wild ones that had never known a master and a hearth, understood the meaning of a stick. They could not know that in *this* yard and on *this* night, the wielder of the stick was not a man to do much more than shake it from a distance.

Busi did not expect his current and his only neighbors in the house next door to offer any help or even stir, no matter how much barking there might be. Their rented villa, the Pastry House—once home to a family as celebrated for their baking as Busi was for his voice—was in even greater disrepair than the singer's. The tenants were much younger than him, a careless, cheerful gang of ten; students, he supposed, though he had never asked. They were evidently deaf at night and blind by day, and had scant desire to defend or to protect the yard they shared. Their old neighbor might have lived there all his life, as had his parents and grandparents; he might very well have been born in the same room as the one in which he now slept—but this was no concern of theirs. He was free to love his home, good luck to him; they were free to live their frenzied lives. So Busi was always the one who'd sweep and tidy up, restore the pots of fessandra shrubs—which Alicia had planted—to their pedestals, upright the bins and hose away the pellets and the droppings that the diners had deposited, their satisfied gratuities. One morning, after an especially metallic night, he had even had to drag a neighbor's motorcycle back onto its stand. He'd found it toppled in the yard and had mistaken it, in the half-light, for a beast, a shiny, slaughtered carcass with rubber-ended antlers, bleeding oil. He had been tempted once in a while to post a note through his neighbors' door, asking that—especially—they did not throw out their fish and meat waste without at least wrapping it and sealing it. Certainly they should make sure that the fodder they could not eat themselves should not be too easily retrieved by animals or settled on by flies. But he kept his grievance to himself. He had a reputation to protect as a calm, distinguished man, a man too tranquil to complain. Besides, he was a little nervous of the young, never having had a son or daughter of his own, never having had a sibling either.

There was a further reason, though, why Busi wanted to be armed, if only with a gentler weapon, a reason that defied all reason. He had never been keen, not since he was a child in this same house, to walk out onto the landing in the dark. The family home was disconcerting after dusk. It was not a settled building, despite its age, and had its own percussions, which for anyone with an imagination were as alarming as any beasts might be. It was constructed in the craftsman style, hand-built to have a bit of play-and-give in every joint and seam. Even the bulky painted paper on the walls was leafy and loose; it smelled of either sand or salt, depending on the season and the tides, and was irreplaceable, an heirloom in a way—but it was also all that stopped the aging plaster daub from crumbling. So it stayed and helped to absorb and soften the unrelenting racket of the house. The villa's timber frame and floors, the stairs and banisters in inlaid tarbony and lime, the veranda and the balcony, the heavy doors—all muttered, wheezed, and fidgeted like ships, especially on tropic nights like this when the winds were coming off the sea, made vastly muscular by all its distances. Anyone alone upstairs, nervous, fretful, wide awake, might mishear the shifting wood as footsteps, or as an intruder tinkering downstairs, or nosing round, or treading not quite carefully enough on creaking boards. On decks. No lucky child, born into money, and certainly no widower, in fallow days, beleaguered by the dry and shrunken sorrows of a life alone, would return to sleep through that, would not imagine he had human visitors, intent on narrowing the gap between the moderately prosperous and the poor.

Busi, holding what he called his clouting stick at the bloodless, narrow end, stepped out onto the landing, armed, and knowing that he looked absurd. What might those students think if they could see him now? Quiet as feathers, in bare feet, with sleep-encrusted eyes and aching calves, dressed only in his summer bed wear, and feeling frail and foolish, our town's celebrated singer felt his way toward the stairs. It was still implacably dark inside the house. He might as well be blind. The dawn, if there was any dawn so early in the day on flatter ground, had not yet cleared the heights beside the villas to soften the night sky with any of its felted grays. For once the house was entirely free of shadows, such was the saturation of the gloom and the meekness of a bashful moon. There was only creaking blackness and the smell of something he half recognized but could not name just yet.

Busi was not a superstitious man. He had rarely thought that there were ghosts, although the house was eerie—but it was only eerie in the way that caves and woods are eerie, the suspicion that your every move, your every thought, is visible and known to some dark watching life *in there*. For him, the stairwell was not haunted, then, by people who had lived there in the past—by

Busi forebears, say, or servant girls who'd not been treated very well, or suicides. But it was stained, he'd always thought—*colored* is a truer word—by memories. The darkness held and always would the wife that he had loved and lost.

For a moment, Busi considered turning on the lights. There was a switch within easy reach. But turning on electric lights, he knew, would bring the shadows back and, with the shadows, all the glaring clarities of fear. Besides, the light would make him visible to anyone or anything below. Instead, he leaned on the balustrade and did his best, despite his bleariness, to fathom the darkness of the stairwell. He would not risk another step until he could be certain that the house was his and his alone, and that he would not need to square up across the top tread of the flight and strike whoever or whatever tried to come upstairs. But finally, and steadied by the banisters, he started to descend.

If there were any animals outside, they must have heard Busi pulling back the bolts on the heavy kitchen door. He made as much noise as he could. He gave them time and plenty of reason to escape. When at last he looked out into the yard, there was nothing living to be chased away other than the usual gang of thin, disdainful cats; nor was there anything to cause alarm, except for distant movements on the scarp behind the house and in the deeper, flatter forest on the headland. Little more than vegetation shrugging off the wind, perhaps. Little more than natural history.

He stood and waited at his kitchen door with only darkness at his back to lend him company and only his walking stick to provide the courage to proceed, but after a minute or so there was still nothing to be seen or sensed outside his house apart from the smell and the shadow wake of something having passed that way, and recently. He gripped the stick and took a step outside, treading in his naked feet on dew-soaked, rain-drenched flagstones, wet and slippery as slugs. It was only marginally more light outside than in. His toes could feel the debris on the ground, the slime of boiled vegetables, the glop of cake and bread, the maggots and the crud. What could he do in darkness such as this and in bare feet but leave the mess until the day?

He could just make out the outline of the bins. He could certainly smell them, the discarded meals of two households and eleven appetites. It took him only moments to set them upright on their metal feet and to find and replace their lids securely, weighted down by some loose patio blocks. He had already lifted his foot to mount the single step into the kitchen—he was, in other words, committed to the return indoors—when he heard a tinkling of bells. That sound was unmistakable and one that he associated with his wife. Alicia had always been less vain than her husband and not obsessed with what she weighed. What could it matter if she seemed a little plump, so long as she was well and happy with her life? She didn't have to please an audience. She didn't have to run a marathon. She wasn't looking for another man. And so, if she ever felt a little peckish, even in the middle of the night, there was no reason why she shouldn't pad down the flight of wooden stairs to rummage in the larder or in the cool room for a snack. And every time she opened up the larder door, the chain of dainty Persian bells hanging between the hinges and the latch tinkled out its greeting, like the street door of a restaurant. Upstairs, Busi would hear the cheerful and approving sound of hunger recognized and hunger served; he would hear the larder being closed and know that soon his wife was coming back to bed, smelling, tasting, of her snack.

She'd been sweet-toothed when they first met, and then she had become more savory. He'd tasted sugar on her mouth, the honeymooning years; then he'd tasted salt and seasoning, when their marriage had matured. Toward the end, he tasted it even before she reached the bedroom door.

Now he tasted nothing, though he heard the bells. For a moment, he forgot that she was dead and half expected to find her standing at the larder door, grazing on a wedge of cheese, a cold potato possibly, a page of cured ham, some pickle on a wafer bread. There's little in a marriage that is more tender than to meet your spouse out of bed and in the concaves of the night, her body smelling of you both.

At the moment when it fled the riches of his larder and came for him, Busi could not say exactly what it was. Something fierce and dangerous, for sure, something that must have slipped inside the house in the moments when he was setting right the disorder in the yard. But its species? No idea. And male or female? Well, the smell was hardly womanly. The smell could not belong to any bed or any wife. It was neither sweet nor savory. No, it was pungent, lavatorial at first, and then much flatter. Not a bad smell, actually. Not excrement. Not sweat. More a mix of earth and mold and starch. Potato peel. The creature's skin would feel as smooth, as damp, as lightly pelted as potato peel. Naked too. Naked as potato peel.

Very soon, in a second, probably, and at least before the creature's teeth sank into the right side of his hand and, flesh on flesh, the grip of something wet and warm began its pressure on his throat, Busi knew enough to be quite sure that this creature was a child. A snarling, vicious one, which wanted only to disable him and then escape. The attack would be both resolute and fleet-

ing. Busi was still holding his clouting stick, but he did not try
to use it, not even as a lever to prize this animal away, not even
when its teeth had latched onto the singer's cheeks and lips, and
its hands—no, actually, its claws—were tearing at his neck. He
did not use the clouting stick, because, although he recognized at
once the economy and strength in that meager body and its pri-
mordial ferociousness, clearly making the child capable of killing for a crust, he did not truly feel sufficient fear or even much
brutality. This was only turbulence, a storm of moths, a whirl-
ing, snarling halo of damp air. It seemed to Busi—in retrospect,
at least—that he was simply part of something natural, something old and natural and passing. This wasn't personal. They
were not enemies. This wasn't even human, in a way. There was
no sentiment or conscience, nor any anger or psychosis in the
bite or in the grip, though they were damaging. Nor any greed.
Nor any immorality. There was only hunger and the sort of fear
that any animal might have if startled by a looming body while
it settled to its food.

A moment later and the child had gone, back through the
door, departing to the tinkling of bells, back through the communal yard, too hurried to be careful with the bins, which
crashed against each other as they fell again, back through the
twanging shrub and scrub of the bosk, back beyond the hill into
the deep, embracing cavern of the trees.

2

THE PHOTOGRAPH OF BUSI in his suit and bandages was first printed in *The Register* and, at the weekend, in *Indices*. Later that summer, it would find its way into the more jocular pages of the *New York Times*, the *Bavarian*, the *London Illustrated News*, *L'Express*, the *Digest of Valletta* . . . and after that? Well, everywhere. Who hasn't seen the photograph? It spread around the agencies and the editorial networks like a summer chill, earning small amounts in fees and causing either sniffs of doubt or fevers of excitement whenever it appeared abroad. Our town's official photographer for civic events had had the sense and foresight to recognize how odd and eloquent it was and likely to appeal to anyone who preferred their stories tall, and so he claimed, not quite within the rules, the reproduction rights. For him, the image became, like Busi's "Babel, Babel" or "The Drowning Sailor Speaks of Love," a source of pocket money for twenty years and more.

The unbecoming image, which was farcical or sinister, depending on the viewer's gullibility, was, in the years that followed the assault on Busi, retouched and lustered for the magazines. What was indistinct in newsprint became sharper and more permanent. Busi's face—though not always his name, which was frequently misspelled or not included in the caption— once again was recognized, even by the young. If he was greeted while walking on the seafront by some stranger, it was just as likely to be because of what had happened at the larder door and, of course, the catastrophic week that followed it, as because of his renown as *Mister Al*. The reproduction that most tourists carry with them even now in the *Bohm & Hannë Travel Guide*—as they set off from the liner port in coaches or taxicabs to ricochet between the seafront and the fort, the basilica and the clutter of the civic museum, the botanic pastures and the souvenir arcades in town, before the long drive out west to the forests and their teeming wildlife—presents the photo cropped, and centered on the face behind the crisp white strips of recently dressed wounds. The caption asks, *Is this the missing link?*, meaning the assailant rather than Busi, of course. What follows is a jaunty anecdotal summary of the "ape attack" on the wounded victim and how it provided living evidence—for crypto-anthropologists through-out the world and anyone else with an appetite for curiosities— that a pocket of primeval anthropoids may have survived in our bedeviled countryside, far out of town. "These pristine forests are now easily accessible to visitors. Guided wildlife tours at dawn and dusk leave daily from the port for an expedition into the woodlands and the clearings of 'Poverty Park,' so named not because of its lack of magnificence or its planted domesticity but because of its unfruitful soil, unfit for plows. There, beneath the ancient canopies, only the most primitive survive. Participants can hope to spot one of the rarest *humans* in the world, the last

Neanderthals perhaps," it concludes, giving contact details and a checklist of other species more likely to be seen and photographed and fed.

But on the morning after Busi gave his speech—he'd managed it, despite his nerves, his headache and his injuries—the singer himself felt neither farcical nor sinister. He spread out *The Register* on the window desk where the light—and a magnifying glass—allowed him to inspect the pages closely, and riffled through the property listings, the court reports and editorials, until he found the photograph that he was hoping for. He did not, for the moment, waste any time reading the account of his inauguration into the Avenue of Fame in the gardens of the town hall, or look for any approval or otherwise of how his speech had been received. He was not concerned that the combination of his formal suit, the medals on his chest and on his lapels, and the battleground of bandaging across his face, around his wrist, and protruding from his collar would be considered bizarre and undignified.

The picture, reproduced without any cropping, showed the singer throned on a mayoral chair with flared arms, a carved crest and legs sturdier and better turned than Busi's own. At the photographer's behest, he had managed to look as spry and proud as the circumstances—and the bruises and the smarting wounds—would allow. It didn't show that, on top of everything else, Busi had that morning, on his walk up to the town hall gardens, received alarming news from one of his unhelpful neighbors. He held a reasonably convincing smile. The leather tube that he was gripping as tightly as he had gripped his clouting stick just hours earlier contained the calligrapher's citation for the Worthiness Award he had just received. The chair was placed strategically beneath the recently unveiled marble plinth and a newly cast bust that showed *Mister Al* with his head thrown back in song. The top of Busi's living hair was almost brushing his bronze chin. The sculpture, it must be said, was—on this one occasion, at least—a better likeness of the man than the man himself.

It was another face that Busi was looking for, however. And not the face of the young businessman standing on the right side of the chair, smiling too readily for the camera and with one hand on the singer's shoulder, not quite restraining him. That was his nephew, Joseph, the one who was so keen his uncle should acquire a maid and lodgers. And a shotgun. He had already repeated the suggestion twice that morning. His uncle could have seen off all the troublesome beasts at his door with a single shot, he'd said as soon as an embarrassed explanation for the bandages had been demanded and provided, and there'd have been no wounds to dress—at least, not human ones. "You ought to organize yourself more thoroughly," he'd told Busi finally. "Read your letters, for example. Stay in touch. And try to answer them." A strange non sequitur.

Busi could not find it in his heart to love or even like the *boy*. It was Joseph's mother, Katerine, Alicia's elder sister, who brought Busi closer to the page. In the photograph, she was standing just a little back, leaning without much weight against the plinth, not touching her sister's widower except with her shadow, which draped weightlessly across his shoulder like a shroud. It was not possible to tell from the expression on his face that Busi—not for the first time in his life, no, not by far—was at that moment overcome by a desire, a basorexia of irresistible force, to kiss this woman, this sister Katerine, to press his wounded lips on hers. (I too have felt compulsions of that kind . . . but, no, this is his and not my tale; I'm not the one whose bust is on display among the mayors and generals.)

It was Katerine, or Terina, as she was known within the family, whom Busi had telephoned in the middle of the night, asking for her help. It had not been easy. Physically, that is. The child, the animal, had sunk its teeth into the flesh between the little finger and the wrist of his right hand. He'd had to use his left to dial, and that was testing and demeaning in a way, because it made him clumsy, an added trembling complication to the shock. He had to make the mental effort to redirect his fingers, persuading them to sweep clockwise round the dial on his old and cranky Candlestick Rotary, despite their wrong-handed impulse to do the opposite. His world had been inversed by the attack, he felt, almost in tears. He'd been infantilized, left lumbering and lame and inarticulate. But also he was oddly thrilled, not only by the prospect of his wife's sister taking charge of him in her efficient way but also by the sense that his bruises and his wounds marked the end of mourning. Everything was bound to change or at least loosen. His widowhood would *blossom* now. No, that was not a fitting word. *Ripen* possibly. Or *season*.

She'd found him at the larder door, fussing with the mess of upturned containers and torn packets. He'd brushed spilled flour and some rice into the palm of his uninjured hand and so their embrace was awkward, as he had to hold his one arm wide of her, protect the other, and maintain his body distance too. She was a woman who took care with clothes and would not want her jacket soiled by food or blood. But still it was a comfort to have this likeness of his wife even so briefly in his arms. He turned away at once, embarrassed to find himself aroused. He was bare-footed and in his bed wear, and, though the blood across his face, around his throat and on his hand had stemmed and darkened, it was still sticky—plum sauce—and the wounds were raw.

"What have you done?" she asked, as if the injuries had been his fault, the self-inflicted wounds of someone seeking company and attention. Indeed, she might think so; hers were, he realized, the first words spoken directly to him in at least three days. And then when he explained what he thought had happened at the larder door, she said, "You never saw it, then?" That tone again. And it was true. He hadn't seen the child at all. He'd only had the bite and scratch of it, the smell.

"And did you call the police?" He shook his head; what had happened wasn't criminal. Then she shook hers.

She sat him on the kitchen chair and, holding his chin as firmly as his mother used to when he was a boy, turned his face back and forth, inspecting the damage. "Looks like the work of cats to me. Just surface wounds. Skin-deep," she said eventually, and a touch impatiently. She had been summoned from her bed by *this*—unpleasant, yes, and bloody too, but not quite the severity of injuries that he'd led her to expect. An animal, he'd claimed. But also a child. She shook her head again. "Well, I don't know," she said, which could have meant that she was baffled by the damage to his face or that she didn't for a moment believe his account. "The moggy didn't like you, that's for certain."

Busi knew better than to argue with his sister-in-law. "It truly wasn't cats," he thought but did not say, as she wiped away the drying blood with cotton wool and water and then began to clean the wounds with the same brand of stinging salve his mother had employed those few times when he'd been scratched and torn in the bosk. "Cats or dogs," she said eventually. "You'll need injections anyway."

"For what?"

"For bites, saliva, viruses. Lockjaw, for a start. And rabies, of course. Now, push those lips out. Let me clean your mouth. Can I trust you not to sink your rabid teeth into my hand?" Busi thought that she could not.

Terina played the part of scolding nurse with intimate efficiency, treating the patient as if he were a child, too innocent to mind or even notice the closeness of her body to his face. Busi took the opportunity, or at least did not resist the opportunity, while she went about her restitutions, to sit forward in his chair and rest his hands on her hips. He let her neat and solid torso steady him. And when she applied the adhesive bandages and plasters to the worst of the wounds, he pushed his face into her midriff and let out the kind of sigh that expresses longing more than it conveys soreness or pain. The smell was breathtaking, not just the smell of Terina, which was so meltingly similar to his wife's, but also the vaporous odor of the carbolic disinfectant she had used on him and that, for reasons he preferred not to dwell on, he found provoking, a cocktail of sexual reminiscence.

Busi can be forgiven for his unwonted giddiness. The night had caught him in its swells, dashed him on its rocks, and left him reeling. He could not stop himself from holding her. He could not keep himself from being foolhardy. It had been at least two years since he had even touched a woman or held a woman closely. He was of an age (and still is, he says, despite my hollow protestations) when most people he knew well would rather shake his hand, respectfully, than hug him at the least encounter,

as younger people seemed to do, or kiss his cheek, as used to
be the protocol. Indeed, the last time he'd had a woman in his
arms was at Alicia's cremation and memorial service and, again,
that woman was Terina. Her embraces and her kisses, though,
had been nothing more than dutiful, and appropriate as between
a sister-in-law and a widower. All the mourners were watching
her, inspecting her, of course. How could they not? She had been
dressed so skillfully, so cunningly, he thought, in not-quite-blue
and not-quite-black; a blend of grief, respect, and elegance that
was both modest and conspicuous. He could still remember how
her earrings tinkled like his larder's Persian bells as she took his
arm, when the hearse appeared at the far end of the avenue of
poplars, and leaned toward his face to whisper something comforting. It had been a struggle, after that, to concentrate on what
was being said by the funeral orator and keep himself from eye-
ing her like some daydreaming boy. Alicia would say, if she'd
been standing there, alive, "Terina takes the gold rosette again.
Best mare on show," but with no hint of jealousy or resentment.
Both sisters were content to be themselves, the Body and the
Heart.

Alicia, though, might not be pleased to witness this slightly
swaying tableau vivant in her villa's kitchen in the hours after
the creature's attack. Busi was holding on a little too long, she'd
notice, his arm wrapped round her sister's waist, his nose pressed
into her. It's nothing more than tenderness, he told himself.
But Terina understood more clearly what was going on. It was
a welcome validation in a way that, despite her age—she and
Busi were almost exact contemporaries—certain men were still
allured by her. Mostly married men, she found. In truth, she tried
her best to make it so, not only dressing well but also taking care

to not look withered, holding the line between coltish thinness, unattractive on a woman in her sixties, and wifely portliness, the kind of wifely portliness that Alicia had been guilty of and that she, the elder of the two, considered a surrender to the years. Perfumes were a help, of course. And cosmetics. But her greatest allies were her jackets and dresses, and her shoes. Fashion armored her against the outside world.

Terina did not allow herself to be seen in public before she had found something to look good in, something flattering and costly. Even that early morning, when she'd been summoned from her bed by Busi's frenzied telephone call, begging for her help, she'd found the time to dress properly before the taxicab arrived. No liner slacks or leisure wear for her, no street clothes selected only for their comfort, no workaday footwear. No, the skirt that Busi had wrapped his arm around and the blouse that he had rested his head against, even the belt through which he'd tucked a thumb, were part of a carefully considered ensemble that made the most of her figure, her complexion, and her height. She was—oh, how she wished it otherwise—not tall.

"I think we ought to pay attention to your hand," she said to Busi, stepping back, away from him. She brushed down her clothes at the front, just to straighten them but also to exhibit herself, to let him see the choices she had made as soon as he had called, the grays and pastels she had matched, the naps and textures of the cloths, the cut and movement of her skirt, the softly pressured outline of the body underneath. Materials and fabrics stayed potent, even when the skin was old. Men pretended not to care how women dressed, but actually they cared for few things more, she'd found. Nevertheless, she had not meant to excite her brother-in-law or any man, come to that, in a sexual way. Allurement, yes, but nothing more. At her time of life, bodily conquest was not a principal concern when she was walking out. She was mostly seeking elegance, and hoping to attract the female gaze, with women turning heads to look at her, to notice and approve what she was wearing. Loving clothes had kept her young, she thought. Still, it was exhilarating to be studied with such desire as Busi's, even if the admirer was only her exasperating and familiar brother-in-law. She did not need to look into his lap to see what the effect of her display had been on him. She saw it in his face and heard it in the silence of the room. She felt it on her back when she turned round to fetch more disinfectant, salve, and bandages from the kitchen drawer. Not in a thousand years, she thought, would she ever undress for him, but she could enjoy the fiction, couldn't she, of him undressing her? Being clothed and wanted was so much more rewarding at her stage in life than being had.

It wasn't *wanting* her that was overwhelming and disturbing Busi, but *wondering*, just wondering about the possibilities, the distant and receding possibilities, the *what might have been* rather than the more stirring and heroic *what might be now or in the future*. In recent years, even before Alicia died, Busi had noticed his cravings slowly changing tense. Just as well, he sometimes thought, because at his age maybe looking forward to anything at all was wasteful, futile, and self-destructive. Looking forward was to chase your life away; hoping for the end of winter because of yearning for the spring was to rush the few remaining seasons that were left. Even his sexual life was looking backward now. Especially his sexual life, in fact. Was that the coming of old age, he asked himself, or just nostalgia, a sentimental longing for what was lost? Or was it widowhood? Certainly he could imagine having made love to his sister-in-law in the past, but he honestly could not summon up much belief in their kissing there and then. There were lines that he could never cross, he liked to think. He was not that kind of widower. He was not that kind of fool. In songs, of course, he'd crossed that line a hundred times. He'd sung of lovers and of passion: "Psst, psst, please spare an hour of my time" and "Tarry, tarry; tarry, go." His lyrics spoke of longings, ardors, and desires, all acted on. Offstage, though, his life was unadventurous. *Loyal* might be the kinder word. Busi was not in general an obsessive man, but he was immersive: that's to say, his loyalties ran deep. Betraying them would be against his nature, and maybe against Nature itself. Yet, he smiled and nodded his approval as Terina brushed down her clothes in her affecting way, and still he felt the stirring of his blood. He could allow himself the fantasy of having once been younger in her younger arms.

The soft part of Busi's right hand—the leading hand for any pianist—was more deeply wounded than any of the bites and scratches on his face. It had been torn and ripped almost to the bone. Flat-ended tooth marks were still visible, as was the open-jaw shape of the wound, but it was easy to clean and secure with dressings. Terina pulled up a second chair and sat facing him, slightly to the side, with a towel spread across her skirt. He laid his hand flat on her knee, as she instructed him, and let her clean the wound and apply the salve again.

"Quite a cat!" he said. "A cat with dentures, by the looks of it." He was still pondering what the chances were—no, what the chances might have been, so many years ago, if only he could hijack time—of his sister-in-law salving him in other ways than this. She'd done it, or something like it, once before in his dress-

ing room after a concert, but that was many decades past, when
they were young and unencumbered by the world, and before
Terina had introduced him to "my not-so-little sister."

"You're fixed," she said, stepping back to admire her work.
Only the damage to his upper lip—his singing lip, the one he
arched so memorably, when he tamed and coiled a note—was
still readily visible. Lips are hard to mend and dress. Terina had
only cleaned the wound, but it was swollen now and raw. The
bloody gash had blackened in strange and clashing contrast to
the quilt of surgical plasters that, almost comically, patchworked
his face.

"I look a fool; I'll look a fool tomorrow," he said. In six or
seven hours he would have to face the honor party in his suit and
make his speech.

"You'll seem like a battle hero, a military man, like all
the others on their plinths." They laughed at that: *General Al.*
The generalissimo. "Joseph and I will both be there, of course.
We can guarantee polite applause. Now, is there something; anything . . . before I go?"

Is there something, anything? That was a phrase he'd heard
from her before. An awkward phrase, he always thought. A tease.
Was it a calculated provocation now, a veiled invitation? Busi
wasn't sure—except he had always suspected everything that
Terina did or said was a provocation, calculated or not. She did not
speak, or sit or rise, or leave a room, or join a group, or depart,
without the evident desire to create a stir. So, was there something, anything? What could she have in mind? What was she
hoping for? The woman was a mystery.

Terina raised an eyebrow, evidently baffled and amused by
his silence. "Speak," she said. He lifted his chin to look at her,

but hesitated for a moment more. What might she think and say if he suggested that she stay the night, or what little was left of it, "just for the company"? If only for the company. He could make up the spare bed in a second room or offer her his own bed, disturbed and rumpled though it was, while he slept on the reading couch. She could at least stay until breakfast, even if neither of them tried to sleep. They could sit behind the balcony window and watch the daylight lift and plow its furrows on the sea. The view was better and more stirring if appreciated in company. She might even hold his hands again. It was possible, of course, though he was rusty in such matters, that something more wifely and more tender might occur, something sweetly innocent, something sociable. What he wanted most, of course, was not to spend another dawn alone.

"Do you remember?" he said finally, surprising himself. "Do you remember that one time, the night I sang 'The Pungent Rose' and you came back behind the stage?"

"I don't remember it." She had caught at once what he was referring to.

"You don't remember it?" He sang the last lines of a verse: "I will obtain a kiss / Before she goes / That is my goal / Cajole her with the pungent rose / That's ready in my buttonhole / On nights like this." It had always pleased him that he'd managed to work in the words *obtain* and *cajole*. Other writers would not risk that level of formality. "Does that ring any bells for you?"

"Should I remember it?"

"Should I remind you? Better not."

Now they both smiled, but to themselves, not looking up, not taking any further risks. The hazard and the impulse had now passed. Busi could not read her mind, but for himself he understood that getting older was not so bad so long as he could at least think young. He also understood—and not unhappily—that nothing untoward, nothing out of shape, let's say, nothing gauche and physical could or should occur in this, his wife's beloved house. He would have to take his chances somewhere else, find a little pied-à-terre, perhaps, a hotel room, if he truly wanted love again, if he truly wanted to be free of love. He was still smiling when the taxicab arrived to take temptation—its skirt just slightly stained with Busi's blood—back into the retreating darkness of the town, bringing to a close this most unusual of nights.

*

By the time the first hints of dawn had unburdened the sky above the scarp to the rear of the villa and the wind had given way, making room for the day of his inauguration into the Avenue of Fame, Busi was already bathed and dressed, though not yet in his public suit. It—together with the bar of medals—was laid out on the bed, as tucked and lifeless as a mannequin. He had not tried to sleep after Terina left. What rest could he expect? Instead, despite the early hour, he sat at the piano in his practice room and, in the semidark, attempted some simple exercises. Mostly he was keen to discover how steady his hands were and how much the right one had been injured and impaired, but he also needed to reclaim the rooms and stairways from the night with sound, no matter how clumsily he might be forced to play. The villa felt more perilous than ever before.

His hand did not hurt as much as Busi expected, wanted even, though it was stiff and smarting. Some fluidity was lost;

his fingers were slow in yielding their full range; extending wide for chords was uncomfortable and tugged against the recently tightened dressing. He'd thought it would be wise to stretch his hand and fingers before the scar tissue hardened and became inflexible, but maybe he was causing more damage, reopening the wounds. Still, he wanted to be lamed. He wanted something lasting, something physical, that he could show in weeks ahead to mark and prove what had happened in the night. Terina's amused reaction had unnerved and irritated him. Cats, indeed. A cat was like a carpet to the touch, tightly woven, deeply piled. He knew that human skin was variable, not always clean and sensuous or glossy like a piece of sheeny cloth, not always lightly warm like Terina's own skin, but sometimes clammy, chilly, patchy, like potato peel. But it was never carpeted with fur. He'd have known the difference. His wounds could be the evidence that this was not the work of cats. He flexed his right hand to induce some pain and persuade himself the injury was serious, especially for a man who played piano for the town and now, quite possibly—though this was only pity for himself—would never play as dexterously again.

After a few bars, Busi rested his right hand dramatically on the raised keyboard lid and played only with his left, the more profound and melancholy notes. The boards and timbers of the villa shuddered with the pounding of the keys, absorbing and amplifying it. The deep tones are the ones that travel best and travel farthest, in a wooden house at least, though in the open air it is the highs that fly. When Busi had practiced early in the morning as a younger man, both playing and singing, Alicia, still half asleep, had often commented that it was the bass and baritone that shook her awake and not the treble and soprano of the melody. Busi could imagine her in bed right at that moment, sensing those low notes and not the least perturbed by the absence of the right-hand higher ones. Sometimes, on her brightest days, she'd sing along, a distant contralto, though she could not claim to have the best of voices. She was always singing, actually, songs she'd brought back from the cinema or café matinees, songs that Busi couldn't like but loved to overhear.

He closed his eyes and played some more, in darkness. Now everything was as it ought to be. He added weight and volume to the notes. He forced their passage blindly up the stairs, across the landing and into the bedroom, to the pillows where she lay, two images of her: the first one breathing, waking to the notes, and the second one quite dead and deaf and out of reach. How he wished that he could still *cajole* a kiss from her, that he might *obtain* her love.

Now—almost tearful, for the second time that day—he left Alicia in ever-ending peace and pushed the music, peckishly, out along the corridor into the kitchen and close up to the larder door. Could he with his left hand shake awake the tiny Persian bells and induce a jingle of response, though whose response he did not want to guess? He'd bolted the door into the yard after the attack, of course, but he could not discount the possibility that there was still an animal inside, now trapped, bewildered and precarious. What would an animal, a child, that had never encountered the music of instruments before make of the somberness, he wondered, the cave and thunder sounds that were now coming from the singer's fingertips? He had to open his eyes to blink away the thought. What might have happened, say, three years earlier when Alicia was still well, her appetite unweakened, if it had been she who had descended in the middle of the night, unarmed, barefoot, quiet as feathers, with sleep-encrusted eyes, to find a snack to feed on and then discovered, as Busi had done, only hours previously, the creature at the larder door? The brute. The beast. The cat that had no fur. The child. The aboriginal. Busi would have heard from their bed the high metallic notes of Persia, the right-hand music of the chain of bells, the street door of a restaurant, and considered it entirely normal, another married night in love, and soon his wife would return to him tasting of her food. Or else—the nightmare rather than the dream— she would return to kiss him with her torn and bloody lip. Or else he would have to hurry down himself to discover what had delayed her for so long at the larder door, and he would find her crumpled on the floor, a gaping wound across her throat, her skin as cold as tiles.

The idea for a new song came to Busi, brought back to the piano by the low notes he had played and by the high notes he had hoped for in response. "Persian Bells," a wounded, tinkling lament for . . . well, it was hard to be quite sure which of the two would be the object of his pity. The wife or child? Both, possibly. He returned his injured right hand to the keyboard and, resting his left hand now, found the sequences that most resembled bells. He teased a phrase that might reveal a melody, if he worked on it. Would he find the energy to work on it? He hadn't written anything worthwhile for a year and more, so why continue now? He was aware that whenever in the recent past he had announced in concert that the next song was a new one, there was more regret in the room than excited expectation. His audience had come to rendezvous with music that they knew. His repertoire was like his sex life nowadays, retrospective, elderly. They'd rather hear his foolish, playful ditty, "Love is like / A motorbike / It needs two wheels" or laugh along with "Where We Were Tomorrow" or join in the choruses of "It's a Case of Do or Die" than tolerate his latest, mournful "Persian Bells."

Despite the soreness of his hand, Busi chased this latest phrase a little more along the keys and thought that it was promising, though whether it would be a love song for his wife or something wilder and more savage—the bedroom or the larder door—he still could not tell. A lyric might provide the answer, but that would come only with singing, and Busi could not sing or exercise his voice just yet. His upper lip was certainly too sore for that. Too sore for talking, at the moment. Too sore perhaps for making that damned speech in only a few hours' time. Too sore for eating, that's for sure. Too sore for kissing? Absolutely, yes. He shook his head again, to dislodge the memory of his sister-in-law and her recent ministrations. It kept on coming back, even though he was now dressed and sobered by the lifting light, the dawning of this worst of weeks.

What if Terina had responded to his almost-spoken importunities and stayed with him that dawn, *just for the company*? There would have been no kissing, not a peck. There'd have been no true tenderness either. He'd known his sister-in-law for far too long to imagine there could be anything profound between the two of them except a gulf, but there had always been a frisson when they met, an echo of those moments in the concert dressing room when, after what had been the briefest of liaisons, she had—only playfully, she would claim, and for the boast that she had been with *Mister Al*, the celebrated singer, and collected more than his autograph—loosened his trouser top and pushed a narrow hand with its long nails and its unforgiving rings under the band and into his underclothes. Nothing in his life, his intimate life, that is, before and since, had shocked him quite as much as that. Or frightened him. No matter what his songs might claim, he was not experienced in matters of seduction. Even then, her attentions had been clinical and nurselike, unengaged, indulgent, and amused. Afterward, baffled by the coolness of their interchange, its lack of generosity, he'd casually—no, carelessly—invited her to join him the following evening for a walk along the promenade and then an aperitif in one of those shadowy bars, long since demolished, where the sailors and the conscripts used to wait the call. That was the least, he felt, that he could do, by way of thanks. He was in debt to her. But she declined, as he had meant her to.

"Now, is there something, anything . . . ?" she'd asked that night of "The Pungent Rose," standing at the dressing room's half-open door and brushing down her clothes.

He'd never quite deciphered what she meant by that uncompleted phrase, not then, not now.

"No, nothing," he'd replied, too readily. She had embarrassed him. And actually—although she'd never admit it, even to herself—he had offended her.

Terina's retreat from him that night at the concert hall, from Busi's point of view, was as sudden and unnerving as her forwardness. That had been her plan, he always thought. She was a beauty in those days and must have been exhilarated by the effects she could produce in men. She might leave them breathless with a glance. She could both provoke and meeken them with just the folding of her arms or the crossing of her legs, or—a habit of hers that Busi remembered well—by resting the tip of her tongue on the gable of her upper lip. Men were arrested by her every move. She would surprise the lucky ones with her obliging hands, Busi supposed. He doubted he had been the only one to suffer that.

Yet she was also wildly chaste. She had her etiquettes with men and her procedures, none of which disturbed her clothes or smudged her lipstick or her rouge. None of which—and here's the point—involved a contraceptive or any hazard for herself. If Terina was a woman who "feasted" on male weaknesses, as Alicia had claimed, not disapprovingly, her elder sister had no ordinary desire for getting truly close to men. Her sudden marriage—to Pencillon, the timber merchant, more than twenty years her senior and in rapidly declining health—had baffled everyone. It took place the summer after her brief entanglement with Busi in his dressing room, but it didn't last much longer than a year before a heart attack put paid to it and to him. According to the gossips and corroborated by the two maids who worked for the household, the marriage was never consummated. They reported, memorably, that the couple hadn't even shared a bathroom or a bed, let alone "the goo-goos" or "endearments." The merchant had "no timber" when it came to love, they said. Mr. and Madam Pencillon stored their dirty towels, clothes, and sheets in separate laundry baskets with instructions that the contents should not mix even in the copper used for washing.

But if the pair of them had never "shared," that meant, according to the wisdoms of the street, that Joseph, Terina's son, had to be the product of a man other than the ailing merchant. Alicia, however, was always insistent that it wasn't so; the husband was obviously the parent of the merchant-minded boy, she said, never mind how that had come about. Separate laundry baskets notwithstanding, Joseph had the merchant's lanky, heavy build, and the same inflections when he spoke, despite his father having died before his son was born.

Nevertheless, there were many men who, out of earshot of their mothers and their wives, liked to imply that they could have been Joseph's father themselves . . . discretion, please; they would not reveal—ha, ha—the *ins and outs* of what had happened in that bed or car or hotel room. Others thought about it, hard and long, thought about the joys of lying down with Katerine Pencillon, thought about the ecstasies of having her, imagined resting their own tongue tip on her enticing, gabled lip. And, inevitably, there were some who linked the names of Alfred and Terina romantically, and never doubted who the father was. They'd heard that, on one occasion at least, the singer with the Feathered Voice, the Chanson Dove, had employed the sedatives and aphrodisiacs of his disarming songs to be intimate with chaste and lovely Katerine, in his concert dressing room. If once, why not a dozen times, they asked themselves, why not repeatedly behind the timber merchant's back?

Busi had met Alicia by the time the rumors were most prolific, and if she heard them she did not mention it to him. He'd known the child, Joseph, of course, a tall, demanding boy, early to walk and quick to talk, with abundant dark hair and a passion for collections, for coins, stamps, and lepidoptera. They had been close. Once in a while, when the sisters were having lunch, perhaps, Uncle Alfred and his nephew might have been seen together on expeditions in the town or at the Tax Museum, as it was known (the Institute of Taxonomy and Taxidermy). Uncle Alfred did his best to help. Yet nobody could truly think that clay-haired Busi was the father. He'd hardly touched Terina, after all; the touching had been done by her.

Had Alicia ever known about his single, hurried, one-handed liaison with her sister? Busi doubted it. He had at first judged it wiser not to tell her. The details did not flatter him. Later, though, with their marriage so readily secured, he had counted his secrecy to be a mistake, now too late to remedy. Of course, there was always the lingering risk with Terina that if an argument flared between the two sisters, the slender and the plump, the elder might throw in the grenade of how she had been importuned when she was still an innocent young woman, a trusting fan, by Alicia's philandering husband, her none too blameless *Mister Al*. To have confessed the brief encounter to his wife years ago would have lanced that danger, of course, and removed that one anxiety. But Busi was a cautious man. Prudent, he would say. Discreet. How could he ever admit, "Your big sister played with me the once. I blush to think about it still (and yet I think about it all the time)"?

Now, with the first sunlight of the day sheening out across the piano top, Busi tried to focus again on his exercises, to see if he could coax the new melody of "Persian Bells" into a more touching progression of notes and tones. The effort was too much. His concentration was blistered—blistered by the child as well as by the past—and he was weary from his almost sleepless night.

Once more he mounted the stairs to the landing, where that morning he had hesitated in the blinding darkness. Now the shadows that he feared with all their depths, their contours, and their shapes were stretching long and low across the flights and out across the landing. Nighttimes he could cope with. Sunlight too. But these shadowed mornings, meanly lit by the ascending day, were often more than he could bear. Not quite the morning. Not quite the night. But that gray and docile hour in between, when only weather should be making noise and only deadly sins are busy on the streets.

Again, he took hold of his clouting stick and peered into the corners of the rooms and underneath the tables and chairs. He had to check in every place, to be sure he had the villa to himself and that the building was his and his alone. He was ready to square up and strike whatever tried to come at him.

*

The house could not be emptier. And, as far as he could tell from the little window in the first-floor bathroom, the downstairs yard was empty too. He might have liked to catch a glimpse, a calmer, reassuring, bloodless glimpse of that small child, but there wasn't even a single cat, soaking up the damp, on his yard's flagstones, or any birds, or any rodents drinking at the drains or filching from the bins. He pressed his ear against the glass and heard the bosk, the fractious groaning of the trees, the chanting of the shaman toads, but little else.

The bedroom was the last place to be checked for animals or any naked child. He still could not enter the room at that time of the day, his piano exercises completed, without projecting a memory of Alicia, sitting up among the pillows while he presented her with a pot of coffee, warm brioches, and an apricot or stem of grapes. "I know exactly how to excite and satisfy a woman in bed," he liked to say. "Breakfast on a tray." That morning he could not help but think the opposite: that actually, despite his age, he had never understood how to satisfy a woman sexually. Not even Alicia, perhaps. Was it too late to be a player on that stage? With someone other than Alicia? He recalled a musician he'd once known, a trumpeter, who'd tried in later life, when his breathing let him down, to switch to the accordion. "It was adultery," he said. "I never learned to master it. Too late. Too old."

The final space that Busi had to check, for peace of mind, was underneath the bed. Rather than bend or kneel—he was too stiff and unsteady; God save his joints—he rattled his stick about in the quilt-protected darkness, only for a moment fearing that a pair of hands might thrust out to grip him by his ankles, only for an even briefer moment wishing too to find the child cowering there so that it might be tamed and fed and civilized, adopted even, cherished. If men and women can be besotted by a cat, despite its untamed claws, or adore a dog, despite its savage teeth, why not a child, no matter that the child is wild? All he located were suitcases, boxes of sheet music and the snagging elastic of spiders' webs. He shook his head at his own foolishness, and at his loneliness. The sooner he left the house and stepped into the street, the better. Let the day begin.

His best day suit, a noble blue, fitted just a bit more slackly than it used to. He could run his hand below the trousers at the waist quite easily, and they were baggy at the back. He had to cinch the waistband firmly with the buttons at the side. His neck, he thought, looked scrawny at the collar, especially once his tie had been knotted, and the shoulders of the suit were unusually loose. He felt more spirited now that he was fully dressed, however. All that remained was for him to drop his fossil talisman into his jacket pocket for good luck and select the medals he would wear, his row of polished vanities. He had a drawer half full of them. It was the lazy habit of the town and had been for several hundred years to hand out these decorations—to men, that is—for anything achieved, no matter how minor or mean—for the completion of a building project, say, or for lifelong service with a restaurant, or a golden wedding anniversary. Wearing them was to publish on your chest a shiny, brief biography.

Busi's chosen biography that morning of his speech declared him to be a member of the Trojan Public League, a forty-year supporter of the citizens, as well as an honorary doctor at the Music School, a category winner at the Athens Festival of Song, and our associate ambassador for the arts at galas and symposiums around the world. He clipped the five decorations to his lapel and turned toward the full-length bedroom mirror, something that was rarely used these days. No, nothing he could do or wear would mask the presence of those dressings and those bandages, or hide the swollen, bloody bogey of a scar across his lip. Actually, he didn't mind. They were his visible excuse for making a poor speech or stumbling with his words of thanks. People would be alarmed for him, and would beg him for the details. Cats were not involved, he would explain, making light of his experience. Nor any other animals. It was a hungry child that had attacked him. No, more exactly, it had been a boy. He knew enough about our town and our automatic ribaldry to want to shut down straightaway any likelihood that he'd been scratched and bitten by a girl, a fierce and very naked girl. Oh yes, oh yes, we've heard that one before, they'd say. No, it was a child and absolutely had to be a boy. A boy would be the safer choice. He was almost looking forward to the tidy story he could tell.

Alfred Busi stepped out onto the street, leaving the villa not by the yard with its sludge of mashy food and waste waiting to be swept and hosed, but by the high double doors out front with their portentous, weighty key, as befitted someone wearing medals and a suit. It was early. He had time and would not have to take a motor cab or one of those old pony traps still available to tourists on the promenade. He'd walk. It wasn't far up to the Avenue of Fame, even by the longer, safer route along the peopled boulevards and thoroughfares, avoiding the slums and tenements. Busi set off with the sun behind his back, toward the town, treading on his shadow, toeing it ahead. He chose the cool side of the street, close to the shops and offices and already busy with its early chores. He was hoping to be recognized, hoping to be stopped and asked, "Why, is that *Mister Al* underneath those bandages? Whatever have they done to you?"

Indeed, he was soon greeted. He had hardly taken a dozen steps from his door. A square-set, untailored woman, in her twenties, whom he presumed at once to be one of the "students" from across the yard, called to him with more animation than alarm. Oh, how the young love unexpected change.

"It's coming down," she said, and pointed at the villa where she lived, scarcely looking at Busi. As he arrived at her side, she held him by the elbow, with easy, childlike familiarity, but did not address him by name or shake his hand, let alone comment on his bandages, or his injuries, or ask why he was so medaled and so stiffly dressed. She was clearly more eager to pass on her news than to observe more formal social lubricants. But, no, he would not mention her abruptness or reveal any unease by shaking his elbow free.

"What's coming down?" he asked, looking at the unshored

balcony and at the timberwork. Repairs and restorations to the villa—to both the villas—were overdue.

"Our landlord's agreed the sale. It's coming down," she said again.

"Your villa is?" His armpits flushed with sudden sweat. "The whole of it?"

"The Pastry House. It's as good as dust and rubble. I should say, it's only as good as pastry crumbs. Everything's been signed," she said. "And we're evicted. Roofless now." The news was clearly not disturbing her. The town had many other roofs.

"When will this happen? Did they say?" Now he was breathless, and as clammy cold as mozzarella cheese.

"Not long, I think. Oh, I don't know. They didn't want to talk to us. Before the sledgehammers and the dynamiters get to work, let's hope. There'll be compensation, don't you think?" Again she took his arm, as if they were old friends, and awarded him a rueful, impish grin. "No pay, no play; no pay, we stay." He could tell that she was searching for another slogan or for further rhymes. He'd made a living out of finding rhymes.

Finally, she let his elbow go and mimed the coming demolition with an explosive puff of her cheeks and an emphatic spreading open of her palms. The sun, which had been hidden by a brief scarf of cloud, emerged the moment she finished speaking and spotlighted both the villas' frontages, as if she'd summoned more dramatic lighting with her explosions and theatrics. "A pity, though," the woman said. "They're nice-looking buildings, aren't they, in the light?" And then, at last, she turned and stared at Busi, maybe even sensed her news had wounded him. "Whoops-me!" she said, half to herself, and added, "What have *you* been doing to yourself?"

Busi no longer had sufficient heart or energy to answer. He could only stand at his neighbor's shoulder, looking up toward the buildings and the bosk and the prospects of a steep, blue day, eager to regain his breath and normal temperature, and then escape toward the Avenue of Fame. Behind their backs, the sea persisted, dragging shingle from the beach, picking at the high-and-mighty shore.

3

SATURDAY WOULD BE CHALLENGING. It might start and end in pain. Busi jotted down his list of the day's errands and appointments. He could wriggle out of all of them, except the final one. He had agreed, as a coda to his inauguration on Wednesday, to perform an early-evening concert in a marquee in the gardens of the town hall beyond the Avenue of Fame, where his bust was already whitening with dove and pigeon lime, life's streaky bandages and dressings; now it began to look more like the man himself. This would be a dutiful event, ticketed and stilted, for dignitaries and civic notables and not one for aficionados. The general public could attend, of course, but we—yes, I was on the fringes of that crowd—would have to stay outside and listen to the music blindly, sitting on the lawns and garden walls. Busi hoped that *Mister Al* could perform entirely free of bandages.

First, though, he meant to buy himself a copy of that week's *Indices*. There'd be another photo and a longer article about his speech and the unveiling of his bust. Before the ceremony, he'd given quite a lengthy, nervous interview to one of their more seasoned and more lively journalists—a writer who hid behind the amusing soubriquet of, well, Soubriquet—and had, as intended, taken the opportunity to set the record straight about his injuries: a naked boy and not a cat, nails not claws. He feared he might have been too open with the man. Busi always treated others as he would like to be treated himself but seldom was. It would be interesting to see what the magazine had made of the attack, but most of all what Busi was expecting were some paragraphs of praise. This was something to look forward to. He'd go into the market arcades after his call at the newsstand and see if he could spot a little gift for Terina. He'd roused her in the middle of the night earlier in the week to fix his wounds, and she had not complained. She had, in fact, been calm and kind. Some costly gratitude was overdue. He knew of a draper's where he might buy a scarf for her. He thought a patterned saffron silk might suit her well. He'd like to see her throw it round her shoulders and her throat. He would have liked, he thought, to have seen her dressed in saffron, head to toe, when they were young and he was unattached.

*

For lunch, Busi would take his preferred corner table in the little garden restaurant at the town's botanic pastures, and settle back to read and drink and, perhaps, jot down the titles for the evening's repertoire in the margins of a menu, the lonely diner with his back against the decorative hedging. But, in some respects, sitting there alone was not to sit without company. It had been Alicia's favorite lunchtime restaurant. Eating in a garden in the open air—their table nearly always gleaned by the finches and the sparrows, even gulls and butterflies—never failed to brighten her. In fact, they'd courted there, had first professed—confessed—their loves.

"What shape of love is that?" he'd asked that first time, meaning to disguise his mixture of embarrassment and joy.

"Long. Wide. Deep," she'd said carefully, and teasingly. (That was a song he hadn't finished yet, though he'd practiced it on her.)

"Ah, like the Danube?" He remembered what Mondazy wrote: "The Danube that is romance, running Black to Black, from the Forest where it rises to the Sea-shore and the wrack."

"Like a sewer," she corrected him. "Deep, long, and wide, and full of . . ."

"Like a sewer" had therefore become their secret, joshing shorthand for devotion.

It saddened him even to think about it now, and maybe that was why his visits to the garden café were so infrequent. Normally he'd use the public food stands on the promenade, a short stroll away from his front door, in the summer, in the light. The sun itself was company. He had grown reluctant to cook for himself. A meal for one is flavorless. Of late, he was too often eating cold and on the hoof, like an animal, dining from the packet or the tin, too unmotivated to prepare a pan or lay a table. And he had become sadly familiar with the night light of the larder, that bluish light that had no warmth. He had to hold and still the Persian bells when he pulled back the door in case they sounded and left him even lonelier.

But, first, before the arcades and the café in the pastures, Busi had to go, reluctantly, to Dr. Bandel's clinic. Among the fears and worries, the embarrassments, that had unnerved him since the larder attack and the news on Wednesday morning that the Pastry House was coming down, Terina's seemingly playful warning was the one that now seemed most pressing. "You'll need injections," she had said.

Busi had not thought it likely that the child, so evidently innocent, so clearly without human spite, a victim of the world rather than a vector, could carry anything so vile and dangerous as killer diseases, such as tetanus or rabies. But once he'd checked in Alicia's *Home Encyclopedia of Health and Conduct*, it became difficult to ignore the suspicion that already, just days since the attack, he was displaying nearly all the listed early symptoms of a rabid animal: headache and insomnia, confusion and anxiety, itching wounds and a general sense of weakness. There'd been a touch of fever, even; he recalled how his body temperature had fluctuated wildly while speaking to the ill-dressed student from next door, how his shirt had flooded with sweat, how he'd shivered despite the May heat. He was salivating more than normal too. That was a pointer, wasn't it? So was vomiting. He hadn't yet thrown up any food, but he was feeling more frequently nauseous than could be normal. It might be only paranoia that made him want to heave at just the thought of drinking water, but that was little consolation; paranoia could be counted as a symptom too. Busi had first noticed this latest agitation from running taps and swirling sinks when he had cleaned his teeth that morning. He'd had to remove the brush from his mouth and let the gagging pass. "Hydrophobia," warned the encyclopedia, "is one of the more distinctive indicators of the onset of a *Lyssavirus* and likely to precede convulsions and paralysis."

Busi knew he should have acted earlier. It was three days since he'd been wounded, and all the best advice was that a patient should consult a doctor at the earliest opportunity and face the remedy rather than risk "one of the most merciless deaths that nature can bestow," the muzzles and the straitjackets and then the raging, foaming hours of decease. Nothing could be done, once the virus started to display itself physically, except prepare a coffin and a patch of ground and dribble your farewells.

However, our *Mister Al* was just as fearful of the jabs as he was of the disease, and not without cause. His father had been bitten by a fruit bat fifty years before. It had marooned itself among the family brooms and chain-drive bicycles in the same yard where the bins were kept and where the creatures, even then, came down from the bosk to dine on scraps and drink at drains. It had flapped and arched liked the blackest of beached turbots, desperate to escape, but its strangely plastic wings, both dry and oily to the touch, were far too wide and flat for it to purchase any lift and fly without a helping hand. So Papa rescued it and paid the price: a neat, twin-toothed incision on his fingertip that drew only a tiny bulb of blood.

Busi had been playing the piano—then kept upstairs—when the nurse arrived to administer the antiserum. He could spy across the corridor and through a slightly open door into his parents' dressing room, where his father had drawn up his shirt and was standing facing her, unusually submissive, and with his hands resting on her shoulders. It barely seemed befitting. Busi felt ashamed to watch. Papa was humming loudly to himself— and not the tune his adolescent son was practicing—as the nurse prepared to pump the vaccine cultured from rabbit serum— bunny sap, as it was known—through his stomach wall. Her implement, caught in the bright beam of a surgical lamp, seemed more like the metal contrivance Mama used for piping decorations on a cake than anything medical. Busi could see its needle clearly enough to know it was too cumbersome to be effectively sharp.

His father's pain was undisguised and loud, though Busi did his best not to react to the gasp of shock and the rictus of endurance that followed it. He managed not to miss a note or falter at the keys. What he'd seen was far too intimate for witnesses—such high passion on his father's face, such dark, perplexing agonies. The music—a jaunty setting of Dell'Ova's "Carnival Caprice"—had to seem unbroken. The son could not be caught out by the parent, spying.

The damage to his father's fingertip hardly warranted a dressing and healed within the hour, but the bruises on his stomach were mauve and livid for a week, before they oozed and formed a crust, then browned and yellowed. Papa had lifted his shirt again, after supper on the second day, so that his son could sympathize more fully with his suffering. "Next time, the bat will have to manage on its own," his father said. "On the whole, I'd rather die than have that stuff pumped into me again. That woman was a plumber, not a nurse."

So Busi reached the clinic fearfully and with another symptom of infection—shaking hands. He was too early for his appointment. He waited on the waterfront, where our town is most open to the sea and is—be warned—frequently washed and freshened by a salty spray. Courting couples go there to get wet. Busi would have welcomed a drenching, as that may have been a good excuse for turning on his heels and going home again. But the sea would not oblige. It left him dry and warm. He sat on a wrought-iron bench with other men of his own age, drew courage from the sun for the ordeal ahead, and tried to settle his nerves by watching the children and their parents queuing up in the basilica close to ride the hot-air balloon. They'd see for once our ocean and our town as bats and starlings do, minimized and patterned like a map. Maybe he should join the line himself, he thought, and escape the needle through the clouds.

More than twenty-five years before, Busi had dared to risk the trip in this same hot-air balloon. He recognized the painted putti on the wicker gondola and the cloudscapes on the canvas envelope, now fattening and swelling with heated propane fumes. The outing—or the "upping," as the pilot called it—had been a birthday gift for his nephew, Joseph, but the boy, at only eight or so, was too young to find much pleasure in it. He'd said the motion and the smell was making him feel sick, and he was alarmed whenever the burners made their asthmatic dragon sounds. Busi, though, had been delighted with the ride. At last he could see for himself why our town had been described by Victor Hugo as "the city with four lungs." We must assume that Hugo too had been aloft and seen the colored patterns for himself. Our four surviving patches of greenery sat like jade gemstones or gleaming emeralds amid a patchwork of roof tiles and a tartan of thoroughfares.

First, to the north of the old commercial quarters, there were the botanic pastures, where, on medieval plague ground considered too tainted for habitation, a thousand species of trees had supposedly been planted in orderly rows (though the field guide could name only six hundred). Then there were the formal gardens near the town hall with their rose borders and their Avenue of Fame; then the Mendicant Gardens, which even then nobody visited, except the poor—you couldn't get a decent vehicle along those steep and narrow streets, with their many steps; and finally, out to the east, the black and thorny lung of bosk, a smoker's lung, claggy, bronchial, too dense to be regarded as either a garden or a park. These were the scrubby woods where cats and demons went at night to take their chances with the barbs.

It would be a fine day by the looks of it, with hardly a cloud and enough of a breeze for steady progress. These young ballooners would be lucky. They'd see horizons that they'd never known were there. Busi recalled that the weather hadn't been so kind for him and Joseph. There'd hardly been a whiff of wind to drive the balloon far from its starting point or to clear the morning fret. They hadn't seen horizons. They hadn't even been able to see through the haze toward the greater, endless lung of countryside beyond our town, the vineyards, the orchards and the family farms, the olive plantations, the lavendaries, the myrtle groves, the clearings, and the ancient woods of Poverty Park. The view was canopied in vapor. But that hadn't been a cause for much regret. It had seemed to Busi then as if our town, with its quartet of green and open spaces and its cacophony of roofs, was all there was to see that day and all you'd ever want to see. It wasn't hard to love this place. The rest was only mist.

Busi's brief contentment was broken by basilica bells, marking the hour. It was time to submit himself to the surgery. He rose more stiffly than was normal, nodded his farewells at his bench companions, and, as he departed, could not help but lift his hand and wave at the children in the queue. He'd wish them all a calm and happy flight, with no one feeling sick. They must have wondered at the old man's bandages. One of the fathers waved back with his magazine and that was deeply pleasing, a simple gesture. Validating. His loneliness was wiped away as readily and fleetingly as steam on a window. The magazine that had been waved at him was *Indices*.

As it happened, there was a copy of that week's *Indices*—nicknamed *Indecencies* by its devoted readers in recognition of its frequent, shocking candor—in the clinic's waiting room. Busi was tremulous and would have welcomed the distraction of discovering sooner than expected what Soubriquet had written, but the only other patient in the surgery already had it on her lap, leafing through at a craning distance, like someone wanting spectacles. She smiled civilly when Busi bowed and took the chair opposite, but evidently did not recognize the singer or seem surprised by those bandages and plasters still remaining, though peeling and lifting, on his neck and face. An injured man was not an oddity in a doctor's rooms, not even one who seemed so feverish and ill at ease. She raised a handkerchief to her mouth, just in case this other invalid was as infectious and contagious as he seemed, and concentrated on the magazine.

Busi took out the lucky fossil, the perfect *Gryphaea* that he'd retrieved from the forests of Poverty Park when he was a boy, and rubbed its surface with his thumb. It was, commonly, a devil's toenail, valueless, but for the singer it had become, in getting on for fifty years, a talisman without which he could not sing or dare to make a speech or even find the courage to endure the skewering remedy for rabies. The woman in the waiting room—bladder trouble, Busi judged—looked up only briefly from her magazine, squirmed herself more comfortably into her unaccommodating seat, and pressed her handkerchief more firmly to her lips. He watched the pages being turned and flattened—the contents list, a photo essay in black and white of life on board a liner (for the crew), an article about caged birds, another promising the chilling advent of packaged frozen food and beer in metal canisters, a profile of a leading chef (accused of adulteration, both kinds), a page of editorials and cartoons, and then, at last, across the middle spread, the familiar official photograph of Busi and his bust. There was—alarmingly—an illustration of Neanderthals as well, naked at a flaming fire, gnawing bones—men and women and a child. Busi tried to make out, upside down, some of the headings and subheadings in bolder, darker type. He'd not expected there to be Neanderthals—what had they to do with him, "the broker of tranquillity"?—but neither was he quite surprised. Our town was ever full of rumors, all the usual gutter myths, unprovable so undeniable, taken from the far-flung past. "Watch out for ghosts, Neanderthals—and dogs," he had been warned when he was young, as if all three were real and dangerous. It's always so. The sheltered faubourgs and the duller neighborhoods are bound to dream of lives more raw and passionate, less drowsy than their own, the sort of lives of fire and bones that primitive people lived. Busi should have guessed his child would be belittled as *Neanderthal*, a word then used not only for those mythic, untamed mirrors of ourselves but also as an easy insult for any rough and common people living in our town. For many of our residents who never ventured far beyond their neighborhoods, all wildlife was a threat. Cave spiders, cavemen, troglodytes, the vulgar poor? It made no difference. Perhaps Busi had brought this mockery on himself. He'd been a fool to tell this Soubriquet that his attacker had been "innocent and wild." For any shabby journalist in this town, that would be shorthand; it could mean only one thing.

Finally, the woman in the waiting room looked at Busi,

responding to his agitation and to his buffing of what seemed to be an oyster in his hand (so that explained the smell), before returning to the page. Then she looked again, wide-eyed. She'd recognized the dressings rather than the man. "Ah," she said through her handkerchief, pointing at the article, rather than at the subject himself, and pulled a face that seemed to say *Oh, dear!* What she had read of Soubriquet had earned Busi her sympathy or pity. She sat back in her chair and studied him once more. If she had any doubts about the peculiar coincidence of having the person named and shown in the photograph illustrated in the flesh just a pace or so away, they were soon satisfied. The surgery nurse stepped into the room, just as the bandaged man was considering his response to the unvoiced *Oh, dear!* and summoned, "Alfred Busi, please." He was unmasked.

The nurse was not experienced at what she had to do. She had not administered a rabies vaccine on her own before, so she was making an effort to appear briskly reassuring and attentive rather than flustered and unsure. She had seen the article that morning in *Indices*, she said, and sympathized with him. She thought it wise, "in such curious circumstances," that her patient should take precautions, belated though they were. A scratch or bite delivered by an animal was always suspect, in her view, "no matter what the creature might turn out to be." Busi only shook his head, but he presumed her implication was *a cat.* Perhaps— again—he'd been a fool to share with the journalist that there was even a suspect other than the boy.

The nurse read the instruction leaflet from the surgery daybook while Busi undressed to the waist and loosened the top of his trousers so that his stomach was exposed, just as his father's had been half a century previously. He was both scrawny and paunchy under her gaze and awkwardly elderly when she required him to recline on the daybed in the treatment room. He felt unmanned by her, a puny fool, and so he did his best to regain some composure, some dignity, by imagining her as a version of Terina, rousingly efficient and intimate; his friend. But she was too detached to truly take the place of Wednesday morning's nurse. No matter how he stared as she bent over to take the miniature bottle of vaccine from the cold chest and prepare the syringe—happily a shinier and sharper one than his papa had endured—there was no pleasure to be had from her. She was too young for Busi to detect anything sensual or even tender in her proximity. If he were her age, he thought, he would not want to press his face into her midriff or expect to let out any kind of sigh except the sigh that best expresses pain or fear. Desire was not as strong as pain or fear. He would not even want to rest his hands on her shoulders, as Papa had done with such stoical submission, not knowing there was a witness across the corridor.

This nurse was biding her time, Busi saw, more hesitant than decisive. She took her patient's pulse, felt his temperature, and checked his throat nodes for any swelling. "Well done," she said at every stage. She lifted up the corners of his bandages, to satisfy herself that everything was healing. "Well done," she said again, though on this occasion the praise belonged most properly to Terina rather than to her brother-in-law. Her nails, he noticed, when she turned to press her fingers into his stomach to palpate and test his flesh, had recently been painted a cheerful red, then cleaned hastily for work. There were traces of the varnish left beneath her cuticles. Dried blood, he thought at first.

"This is going to take ten days, it says," she told him, peering at the leaflet once again. "One of these a day. We have to alternate the side, so that your stomach wall has forty-eight hours in between to recover from the . . ." She wanted to say, "Recover from the shock, recover from the blunt assault," but stopped herself.

"*Ten* days," he said. "That can't be right. It used to be just one. A single dose. My father had a single dose."

"Well, nowadays . . ." she said, lifting a hand in resignation at the passage of time, and stepped across to brace herself against the daybed. "You'll feel the needle going in. It can't be helped. You must keep still. Try not to tense your muscles. Stay relaxed. I'll be as quick as possible. I have an anesthetic rub that we could try. Best not to watch the actual . . ." Again, she stopped herself. The word she almost used, the word the instruction leaflet used more than once in fact, was *puncturing*.

"Should I turn?"

"Yes, turn your head away, to face the wall if that will help. Think of somewhere that you'd rather be than here. Now, on which side should we start? You choose. Below the liver or the heart?"

As it turned out, Busi would choose not to endure a second puncturing, let alone a tenth. For the moment, though, he tried humming to himself, preparing for the pain by taking refuge in a melody that, at first, he could not put a title to. Of course it was Dell'Ova's "Carnival Caprice" again. History repeats itself; its repertoire is limited. But that was far too jaunty, even for the nurse. She raised her eyebrows, stood away, and waited till she'd quietened him. "Find a picture," she suggested. She meant: take shelter not in a sound but in a place.

Busi did his best to follow the nurse's advice and crowd out his rising alarm by summoning any scene other than the surgery, other than the treatment room's chilly wall, against which he had now pressed his nose, waiting for the cold, metallic pressure of the needle and syringe. He settled very quickly on the public forest to the west, an hour's country drive beyond the outskirts of the town. What made him opt for that, rather than, let's say, the pebble beach below the promenade, where he had played almost every day as a child, or the botanic pastures, where he planned to take his lunch, or even Venice, where he and Alicia had spent their honeymoon, ankle-deep in water—"Like a sewer!"—and beset by smells and love? Clearly, it was the devil's toenail, still in his palm, that had made him think of the public forest. That was where his fossil talisman had been found. Only later would he have a further answer, a storm of further answers. It was the boy, of course. The naked boy. The drawing of Neanderthals. The future of the Pastry House. The bluster of uncertainties that currently beset him. His amplifying fear of life and death. The fact that it was Saturday. His widowhood. All of these were prompting him to take his trepidations once again out to the forests of the west and to the tireless, complicated childhood days that he had squandered there.

*

When *Mister Al* was *Little Alfred*, a boy just starting school, his family's neighbor in the Pastry House started taking him and his own twin sons, Simon and Gilad, Sigh and Guy, out in his rickety horse-drawn van westward from the town to what we now know as Poverty Park but in those days was simply called the clearings. That was where the lumber for their villas had been felled. They went on Saturday afternoons, between the closing of all trade and the coming of dusk, because the baker—Klein, a man of Jewish birth but with little reverence for anything besides his cakes and breads—had to dispose of all that week's unsold stales from his three bakeries and his confectionary shop in town. He could not bear to throw them out, uneaten. "That's sacrilege," he'd said. These solidifying staples of life and these unwanted, fusty treats were, after all, the harvest of his kitchens and his ovens, the products of his labor and his love. He had baked his heart and soul into them. Rather than let them waste entirely, he saved them in a row of basket trays and took them out to feed wild animals. "Hunger lives among those trees," he said. He hoped—though didn't pray—that his weekly philanthropy, his squandering of riches, would make up for his trader's disregard of Sabbath. *Tzedakah* was the Hebrew word he used, rather than the more rabbinical *mitzvah*—a blessing and benevolence for creatures less joyful than ourselves but duller and untroubled. "Eat, bleat, and sleep," he summarized their lives. "And then, come Saturdays, it's bellyfuls of cake. Shabbat shalom."

The three boys traveled blindfolded, in a way, or at least without a sense of where they were. Mr. Klein's fat dog, Honik, always occupied the one passenger seat, while Alfred and the twins rode with the open baskets of stales in the dark rear of the van. The smell was overwhelming, both sugary and sickening, the stench of fungal undergrowth, of athlete's foot, of starch and mold; and then, ahead, from the greater comfort of the driver's bench, the ever-present musty taint of dog, the vapor trail of sweating horses, the clag of Mr. Klein's cigars. There was no cushioning in the van to soften the ride. Unless the three boys chose to rest their backs against the rotting buns and bagels or squat down in the trays among the loaves, they had little choice but to bounce about on the boarded floor like overbaked bread rolls.

The pair of horses kept the van steady on the surfaced roads around the town and on the ridgeway track over Buttress Hill, with its clear views for Mr. Klein and Honik toward the sea, but after that the boys began to tumble and to scream at every pothole and furrow, both in pain and laughter. This is what we want on Saturdays, when school is out—something, anything to paint color on our cheeks. All four cheeks, that's to say. Once they'd reached the uneven and unpredictable forest tracks, a bruising to their buttocks and a cracking of their heads were unavoidable. But Alfred and the twins would not complain. When the doors were thrown back and the boys could clamber out to stretch themselves, the journey was at once worthwhile.

The clearings were the scrubby patches in the forest, too rocky and too thin of soil to support much more by way of interest and color than cistus and genista. Mostly, even in the spring, there were only stones and widow grass—though, when it rained, there could be a spirited and short-lived show of viper weed and yellow day dock, thronging in the crevices, competing for the fertilizing flies. Beyond them on the dipping slopes and in the hollows where the earth was richer and more fulsome, the great dark spreading mass of tarbonies and pepper oaks, tamarisks and pines, casuarinas and carob trees, vied for moisture, light and life, and kept their secrets to themselves. These were the ancient, dripping woods, where no one wise and drawing breath would ever come at night. They were teeming with animals, of course, but they were rich as well with monsters, demons, and the dead, with ghosts and, yes, *Neanderthals*.

Mr. Klein would stand with the horses, holding their reins, in case they grew alarmed at whatever chose to come out for the pastry feast each Saturday. They might bolt if there were swine or scrub boars or stags. They certainly would bolt if there were lynxes or bears. He had the contents of a little pewter flask to keep him warm, and a shotgun, primed and ready, for safety's sake. He was content to let his Sigh and Guy and the nervy Busi boy drag the basket trays out of the van and into the clearings, a distance from the horses.

The boys always begged for the drama of a countdown, so Mr. Klein obliged with the descending numbers, ten to one, before they whooped with pleasure and upturned their treasure troves of food. These were the moments of extravagance that the children looked forward to the most, the tipping of the bakery waste onto the ground. The top loaves, still firm and dry, tumbled out quite readily, but the older ones, the Monday ones and Tuesday ones, at the bottom of the trays, had often become so soggy and congealed during the week that the boys would need to use their sticks to scrape them out, doing their best not to soil their tunics and trousers or gag on the abnormal smells.

Finally, they'd empty out the best basket of them all: the one containing tarts and cakes, the one with strawberries and cream and the whiff of alcohol, the one with the colors and the textures of a work of modern art. They'd spread the contents out into a furring blanket of éclairs, strudels, and gateaux, until the wild pigs, of every genus, unafraid of men or vans on Saturdays, came out of the timberlands, sniffing very fast, sampling the odors of the feast, to gorge on human luxuries. Honik barked at them but did not dare to move.

The boys were glad they had their cudgels for defense,

Alfred especially. His father allowed him to take the villa's clouting stick on these Saturday excursions. (It was that same "gentler weapon" that Busi—ready for the rabies needle now—had gripped so tightly only three nights previously when he descended to his bins.) The pigs were unpredictable and petulant. They did not want to be approached, so being armed was sensible. "Keep close to the van," Mr. Klein would advise, and they were glad to obey, but not because they feared the boars. It was the forest that they feared, its mutterings, its depth, its saturated hollows without light, the stories that had come from it, the stories that retreated there at night.

Dusk was nearly always drawing to a close by the time Alfred and the twins had finished tipping out the cakes, and the various swine had done with eating them. As the light retreated and the body of the forest amplified and dimmed, the boys would scurry back to the van to stand with the horses and wait for any nighttime creatures, tempted by the food but needing darkness. There would be deer, wild cat, and fox, a badger sometimes, weasels too. Once, they'd glimpsed the tumbling shadows of what they took to be a family of bears, and they had seen the silhouettes of stags.

What they feared, but wanted most to see and never did, was one of the wild people said to be the forest's secret residents, the humans who were never tamed but lived on insects, seeds, and worms and, once a week, when finally the van drove off, behind the amber beams of its lanterns, grew fat on bread and biscuits, tarts and cake. Or they would not-quite-hope to spot the people we have loved and lost, the never-dead, the living corpses that existed there, reduced of shape and made as light as gossamer, the ones who—even now—must rest at night in hammocks spun from spiders' webs, the ones who sleep forever on the forest's mattresses of leaves beneath its eiderdowns of mist.

"Honik smells them. Dybbuks. Golems. Djinns," Mr. Klein would tease, lifting his flask to his mouth. "That's why he barks and hangs his tail. That's why I never let him run. He'll track some monkey boy in there. He'll catch a poltergeist. He'll come back to the van with his jaws dripping with ghosts. Which none of us can see. And they have no taste except the taste of . . ." He paused, hit the flask again, and then added, with the chilling certainty of someone who had tasted ghosts himself and would not wish to try them for a second time, "blue cheese."

The last time Alfred accompanied the Kleins to feed the animals—before he begged his parents not to have to go again; he'd rather practice scales, he said, though the pastry man himself had already decided, "in the circumstances," that the neighbor's little Alfred should not join his twins on any future outings—the darkness had descended far too suddenly. The sea had spread a coverlet of thunderclouds across the bed of trees. There had been many diners that afternoon, more than usual. It was as if the creatures needed the comfort of bread and pastries to endure the rain. Crows and ravens shouldered down with their great fabric wings; foxes trotted in, as dainty as danseurs; the few remaining boars were skittish, never liking storms. There was a single, sharp-eared swine. A pair of badgers. Feral ferrets, escapees. Feral dogs. Back-country rats. But you could hardly tell the animals apart. They had become a tumbling swell of hair and bone, once the dusk took charge. The boys could hear the working of their jaws and their babble of complaints, impatient and ill-tempered, mad for crusts and cake.

The boys were relieved when Mr. Klein's flask was finally

empty and he decided it was time to go. "Hurry up," he warned.
"Or else I'll leave you dummkopfs out here for the night, and
let's see what happens. Which one of you will they munch first?"
Alfred had stopped to pick up and pocket his lucky charm, the
Gryphaea, unearthed a moment earlier by the snouting of a boar.
We're told that objects are not powerful. A fossil is inert, as is a
stick. But Alfred Busi, twelve years old and almost adolescent,
knew otherwise. The moment that he wrapped his fingers round
the fossil, he recognized its potency. He did not want to show the
twins or share. This talisman was his alone. It would make him
safe and strong, whatever happened now.

Alfred had almost reached the van and was standing at the
rear, waiting for his turn to jump inside, when something—just a
turbulence, or possibly the fluctuations of a bat—seemed almost
to touch his face. He brushed his cheek, but whatever he had
brushed now seemed to lift and tug his hair, first from the side
and then from behind. It could be fingertips. This was something
that another child might do, the playground bully being weari-
some. But Gilad Klein was already sitting in the cake-free darkness of the van and out of reach. His brother was not far behind.
Whatever was besetting Alfred Busi was something other than
a twin. All that teasing talk of djinns, cadavers, and ghosts, of
golems and Neanderthals, that register of everything chimeri-
cal to fear, had left him tense and ready for the worst. It was a
mixture of the jitters and of instinct, then, an adolescent instinct
now long lost that—in a panic and out of fear that Mr. Klein
meant what he had said about the munching, that demons were
at play, that monsters and the dead had come to take his talisman away—made him swing his clouting stick at it, at them. He
missed. He missed three times. His gentler weapon seemed to

pass through something more than air, and all the more substantial for its nothingness.

This was the first but not the only time he sensed himself enveloped in a swirling and unstable halo of damp air. There was an overloaded smell, a blend of earth and mold and starch and—Mr. Klein had not been wrong—strong cheese. His world had never seemed so treacherous or dangerous. He struck again, his fourth attempt. Again at emptiness. The twins were laughing at him now. The larger of the Klein boys, Sigh, reached out of the van to pull his smaller, irritating friend inside. He too was in a hurry to escape. So were the horses. They pulled against their harnessing and stressed the wooden brake pads on the wheels, wanting to proceed. The odors of the forest were unnerving them, as were the moths. There was a chock-full, flimsy storm of moths assaulting everybody's ears and hair, the dog, the horses, and the Kleins, not only Alfred. The night was pecking at their heads. The twins were mocking him: "It's only little moths, nebish." So Alfred swung his father's heavy walking stick once more. He could not say it was an accident. His violence was now targeted and purposeful. For the first time as a boy, almost a teenager, he gave vent to his savagery and, for an instant, was lost to it. He wanted to locate true flesh and bone. And so he brought the family cudgel down on Sigh's right cheek, baptizing it with blood.

*

In the surgery room, Busi was now clenching his fists so tightly there were nail weals in the palms of his hands. He hardly noticed at first when the nurse drew close to prepare his stomach with a carbolic swab. He was still entangled in that final and inglorious Saturday with the Kleins, and he was in the little bouncing vehicle, with Sigh, the bruised and bloody twin, as they sped back from the trees toward our town, not laughing now, no longer friends, but with the front screen of the van darkening beneath the snow-soft blizzard of the moths, the nattering annual conference of Heterocerae. He was shaking, gagging too. His heart fluttered with unstable fluctuations of its own. Then and now. He felt the pressure on his stomach wall, both of the syringe and the nurse's steadying hand. She took a deep, determined breath, and pressed. The needle broke the skin—a tiny pop—plunged through the fat into the muscle beneath, and piped the vaccine icing into him.

4

SOUBRIQUET HAD TAKEN LIBERTIES. His editor had asked for eighteen hundred "entertaining" words—"Make something of it, Sou!"—and that was far too much for the material he'd been able to gather in the Avenue of Fame. His brief had been to celebrate the life of *Mister Al*, the singer and composer, and to explain to any younger readers who might not have even heard of him why the man was so cherished by his contemporaries and deserved to join the line of colonels and generals among the busts and statues of our town. What had he done to earn his Worthiness Award? Finding out was a job for some dull journeyman, and Soubriquet expected to be bored. It would be a thin event that he might need to thicken at his desk.

As soon as he saw Alfred Busi on the morning of the ceremony, though, walking on his own toward the exalted gathering of available dignitaries, family, and press who had come to witness the unveiling of the bust, he sensed he might discover, there and then, a richer tale to tell, a gory one indeed. The singer was bedecked in bandages. He cut a comic, forlorn figure, with his nose and mouth half hidden, his suit too large, and that vulgar vanity of medals that the singer's generation liked to sport given half an opportunity. Wasn't there a silent movie, a kids' cartoon—Soubriquet could not recall the title—that had a woeful comic *hero* not unlike this tattered man, a walking shaving accident? That was it: "Captain Styptic" was his name.

The man from *Indices* supposed, at first, that Busi was the victim of a fire, a kitchen accident perhaps, especially when he spotted too the bandaging around the wrist and hand. The old chap must have set his cooking oil alight. Soubriquet had immediately dreamed up a neat metaphor about the brief flame of celebrity and a more clumsy one about talent burning out. He was not a writer who kept his distance from the trite or the theatrical. But once he'd introduced himself in the half hour allocated for the interview before the speeches and the unveiling of the bust, Soubriquet learned the truth, or at least the version of the truth that Alfred Busi wanted on the record. The singer claimed he had been mauled at night inside his home by a naked child. A boy, to be precise. He was certain that it wasn't any animal. A cat, for instance. Or a monkey even. He hadn't seen the boy exactly, no. But the encounter had been close and intimate enough for him to feel its skin, its lack of hair, its . . . and here he hesitated at the word *humanity*. "There was no mistaking who or what it was," he'd said. "I recognized the smell of him. It was the smell of children, boys."

Well, that was interesting enough, much better than a blazing pan of cooking oil, but would what Soubriquet had noted down so far fill a two-page spread or could it stretch to eighteen hundred words? He doubted it. No, this would need enhancement, a slick of brilliantine to give the gloss. Fortunately, he had his hair oils readily at hand, drippings from some essay notes he'd made for a piece his editor had just that morning considered "lacking an anchor," meaning it was waffle. Well, waffle lives to serve another day, if you are Soubriquet. Back at his desk that evening, in his unloved apartment shared only by his unloved cat called Sarky, he pulled out those rejected essay notes and placed them alongside the record of his meeting with *Mister Al*. Here was a theme to add some gloss: the theme of "Unrest on Our Streets." There was already in our town, or at least the richer parts of it, a crisis over beggars, theft, and violence, and a general unease . . . no, more than mere unease, a *fear*, the timeless, universal fear of anyone less lucky than ourselves. It was a fear as firmly set in us, Soubriquet supposed (and noted down in pencil), as the corpses of Pompeii were "agonized and petrified in lava." Poverty was the volcano that could very well destroy our town. That would be the writer's thesis. Still hot air, perhaps, and waffle. But now he had the anchor that the essay and his editor required. Alfred Busi, *Mister Al*, could, with a few tucks and a little wipe of oil, be the symbol of a city fearful of attack. What better illustration could there be than all those wounds and bandages? How perfect too that there were medals and a baggy suit.

"Is ur nce c ntented, happy t wn under siege?" Soubriquet asked. His typewriter had lost the letter *o*, both capital and lower case. "Is there a pincer m vement cl sing in n us, armed at ne hand with the usual xen ph bias and at the ther with a nugat ry n stalgia f r the calmer and less lively times that bel ng in st ryb ks m re than they bel ng t hist ry?"

Soubriquet settled at his desk and wrote his four-voweled "Unrest" article at speed. For reasons that were awkward to explain and not easy to suppress, he found the process stimulating. Sexually, that is. This was nearly always how his deadlines were achieved. Impulse, effort, and reward. He would do his best to reach his eighteen-hundred-word target by midevening, then he would walk with the top script and a carbon copy and deliver them to the *Indices* offices at the back of Nation Square, where there were not only bars and restaurants, but also bolt-holes where a lonely, stimulated man who did not like his rented home except when he was writing might lease a woman for an hour. He liked them his own age—that was comforting—or older than himself; Soubriquet was fifty-odd, unmated and apart, and resigned to it. In fact, his ideal rental for the night would be a sporting variant of the woman at the unveiling of Busi's pompous bust. Was she the singer's lover or a friend? It had been difficult to tell. He'd noticed how she'd rearranged the bandages around Busi's wrist. They were close at least, if not exactly intimate. And there was evidently some connection with that dreadful fellow, Joseph something—could he be the son?—who had his spoon in every pie in the town: tourism, finance, property. The business card he'd given Soubriquet at the inauguration identified him, unashamedly, as an *International Trader and Timber Merchant*.

The journalist had slipped the card into his notebook, trying not to engage with the man ("Trade and timber? Such an awful bore") but rather to concentrate once more on the woman, now standing close enough for her cologne to catch the back of his throat. She reminded Soubriquet of an aunt he'd been obsessed with when he was an adolescent. Both were slender, and though unremarkable in height, they were enthralling women, so much more formed and settled than the young, so much more feline and intriguing.

Busi's well-dressed friend had kept herself separated from the body of officials and celebrities, so she appeared in hardly any of the black-and-white photographs that Soubriquet had inspected that afternoon at *Indices* and brought back to his desk. He could make out only her bob of hair and the sheeny shoulder of her artfully tailored jacket in the background of one or two of the pictures. But, even without a closer photograph to study at his desk, he could readily recall her ice-blue bandok, draped across her shoulder as lightly as a snake of mist, and the little colored shoes she wore, with their curved heels. He had especially enjoyed the look of quiet amusement she maintained—and her skirt, the hem, the way it flirted with the breeze, not quite resisting it, not quite succumbing either. It had been hard to concentrate on anybody else.

Now it was hard to concentrate on his piece for *Indices*. Soubriquet had to bring a glass of claret to his desk—with the bottle—and, as was his habit when he worked alone, he undid the buttons on his fly and loosened the trouser waist. For extra breathing room, he'd say. Maybe that was why his article, for all its hurried erudition and its slippery polemic, also managed to seem prurient and as predatory as the *creatures* listed in the text. He wove a story that contained Busi's anxious version of the attack and his certainty that a child had been responsible. But Soubriquet's brilliantined account avoided specifying that it had been a boy, as had been insisted on by the victim himself. The impact on his readers would be more, let's say, *engaging*, if the image they were required to contemplate was of a naked girl, her little limbs wrapped around *Mister Al*'s aging ones in any disposition they might care to imagine, her teeth and claws sunk into him, her body feeling damp and spongy and smelling—a detail from Busi's story that Soubriquet relished—of potato peel. To this he added recent news reports of the beggars and the vagrants who—since sleeping out beneath the shrubs and under rags and board was tolerated only during daylight—were obliged to vacate the Mendicant Gardens at night and spill out ("invade," he would say) into the moneyed, decent, warmer districts of our town, hoping at the very least to make a banquet of our leavings, to dine out at the Restaurant of Waste.

Busi had not been the only one to be attacked by homeless, feral vagabonds and starvelings, he wrote, and his villa was not the only home that had been breached. There had been assaults and robberies in once respectable streets, where walking home at night with a wallet in your coat and just a little worse for wear from drink should be a pleasure, not a risk. Women on their own, as well as families, had been importuned by indigents, demanding gifts and favors of every kind, including some that were too unlikely to describe. Tourists had been bothered and assailed. Traders had been forced to strengthen their defenses. And there had been a spate of burglaries. Again, Busi was not the only man of late who'd had to go downstairs in the darkness of the night to see off intruders with a heavy stick and a pounding heart. And he was not the only one to have scars to show for it. Something should be done to stop the rot ("s mething urgent, s mething sweeping, s mething radical"); otherwise our town would be controlled not by the police but by a tribe of snarling city savages, of "garmented bipeds," for whom our modern streets and alleyways would become what ravines and tracks were to the natural primitives of ancient times: "Their jungle is this t wn."

This was not Soubriquet's own view, of course. He was by nature broad of heart, he liked to think, but not so broad of heart as to muzzle an engrossing story just for the principle. He felt it only right to report, though not with any evidence, that there were moves afoot among the residents closest to the Gardens to take the law into their own hands. The beggars would be driven out of town, together with any other paups and vags who were a bother on the streets. If there were "intemperates" among our townspeople, he wrote, who could not help but see these park-dwelling destitutes as little more than "human beasts wh sh*t and p*ss like d gs," then who was he—a man who, sadly, had no family or wealth to raise a cudgel for—to say they should not also be driven out of town *like dogs* and not encouraged with treats and titbits? He quoted one of Busi's own songs—cleverly, he thought—"The d g y u suppered with last night / This m rning's starving f r a fight," even though Busi's lyric was directed against husbands or lovers rather than any other curs.

Soubriquet needed now to speak to someone from the town's business community, in order to introduce some weight into his report, to represent the man of narrow heart. On an impulse, he shook the business card he'd been given earlier out of his note-book and dialed the number on the cradle telephone his editor had recently had installed for him in his apartment. Yes, Pen-cillon was the name. Joseph Pencillon. Here was "an intem-perate" for sure. Indeed, Trader Pencillon—as he liked to be addressed—took little prompting when he answered the call to share the citizens' concerns as Soubriquet described them. Yes, yes, the town was coarsened, in his view, by all these so-called mendicants.

"And would you further say that they are little better than . . . well, some have told me, they are little better than the animals?" Soubriquet leaned far back in his chair and pushed his spare hand into his fly and underclothes, an invitation—evidently—for Sarky to leap down from the windowsill where he'd been raising the eyebrow of his back at every passerby and test the comfort of his master's lap.

"I'd go that far," said Joseph the Trader Pencillon. "At least that far."

"Like dogs?"

"Like *wild* dogs. Not pets, of course." Joseph had a pair of Maltese mastiffs of his own; they patrolled his timber yard and were, he thought, beyond reproach, unlike the trespassers they caught.

"And might you also have some common sympathy for those who recommend more drastic measures?"

"Such as?"

"Such as . . . I blush to say, but relocation possibly." Soubriquet was glad his smile could not be seen by Pencillon, nor his private parts, which, now that Sarky had decided to stretch out in the hollow of the chair, had all the breathing room they could desire.

"Take the beggars somewhere else, you mean?"

"That's a suggestion, I believe. Relocate them as you might unruly dogs, as you've said. It's well expressed. We have wardens, after all, who round up strays . . ."

"Perhaps those people have a point."

"Relocation might be more humane, better, kinder anyway, than some less temperate solutions," Soubriquet conceded, hardly able to contain his delight and his impatience. Pencillon was leaping into every trap, but there were greater pleasures beckoning that night. "Brute beasts that are a greater nuisance than a pack of dogs might well, I've heard, be treated like a pack of dogs, and whipped."

"Well, I wouldn't favor a whipping. No, not if you have a shotgun or a hunting rifle. A single round of lead should see them off." Joseph had said the same thing a couple of times that morning to Uncle Alfred, and he was happy to repeat himself.

"You see this as a civil war?"

"You do not go too far, I think, but still I do not wish to magnify a problem that need not be a greater nuisance than a midge." Trader Joseph was now testing his mayoral voice; he had hopes of some elected office.

Soubriquet could not help but add, "You do not need to use your hot lead on a midge!"

"Exactly so," our future candidate for mayor continued. "The purpose here is not to shed deserving blood but to protect our growing town before we lose control of it. We should be shaped by wealth and not by poverty. I am a businessman. You have my card?" Businesses—especially tourist companies, hotels, and restaurants—had been damaged, in his view, by all "the out-of-elbows and the down-at-heels" who were roaming wild about the streets. "My uncle, Alfred—he's *Mister Al*, the performer—has been attacked. Just last night. Inside his villa on the promenade," he continued. "You will have seen his wounds already when he spoke with you today. Is this a matter we should overlook? Who is to say a human child will not be next, and with a graver outcome? People ought to arm themselves, protect their properties, or soon our town will be overrun by paupers. A modern town cannot support Neanderthals."

Neanderthals? A gift, a gift. Soubriquet had not only found the commercial gravity, the civic weight, he'd needed to bolster up his article, he'd also found some unexpected added spice. He typed out Pencillon's "immoderate" responses, complete with shotguns,

unruly dogs, and civil war. ("We must h pe this upc ming businessman d es n t truly represent the sentiments f all f us.") He
was at pains to spell the man's surname with just a single *l*: J seph
Pencil n.

Now Soubriquet refilled his glass and turned his focus to the
Neanderthals the timber merchant had mentioned with such a
lack of guile. They had rung bells. Hadn't *Mister Al* made a similar allusion, when describing what was odd about the child that
had assaulted him? It had been both "inn cent and wild." Neanderthal, in other words. A happy pattern was emerging. The
article had grown purposeful—and entertaining. Neanderthals,
indeed. These were the creatures who connected beasts to man.

Soubriquet scanned his notes to remind himself of exactly
what the singer had said. And there it was, recorded in dark-blue
ink and incontestable. Busi had spoken of the trips he used to
take when he was small out to the clearings in the western forests. He'd been teased that there were ancient hominids residing
there. Could it be, Soubriquet wondered now—he'd reached the
home stretch, sixteen hundred out of eighteen hundred words—
that the "girl" who'd wounded *Mister Al* was a survivor of that
clan, an ancient and primeval child who'd accidently wandered
from the trees and found herself dazzled by the daylight of the
town and forced, like so many urban animals, either to seize their
food from open larders or to look for supper at the bins? Could
it be that all the vagrants, all the mendicants, that "Trader Pencil n" would have us point our rifles at were not the *uncivil* but the
uncivilized creatures of the forest, not the town; denizens, not citizens? Might it be a timely kindness to return them to the trees?

Soubriquet raised a private eyebrow at the thought, but the
story was an arresting one that would provide dramatic final para-

graphs, especially if he strengthened it by repeating gutter gossip that he'd heard on and off for years. There were respectable men, it was said (though mostly late at night, in bars), bankers, traders, merchants, mayors—you'd be surprised—who frequented Poverty Park—the clearings that Busi had referred to—and either lured the hominids or forest folk, call them what you want, into the open with gifts of food or trinkets, or else set traps. What happened there might not be rape, but it was bestiality and there were laws to punish that. There were women too, though in the past, admittedly, who, it was claimed, had slept with hominids and even given birth to young, or seminids, as they were known. Then they'd had to convince their parents or their husbands that they had fallen prey in nightmares to the brute attentions of some detested incubus which'd come in darkness to breed with women. They'd not been woken in their sleep. It could have been a moth that pollinated them, the molestations were so peaceable and quiet. They'd only fallen innocently asleep and woken flushed and quickening, their bodies bruised and heavier, their tongues sucked dry. The fleshy evidence was walking on our streets, as large as life. There were youngsters even now who resembled primates more than humans. They were smaller than the rest of us, better to survive the cold, and they were stockier and barrel-chested. Their chins did not protrude, but sat flatly on faces that were oddly broad and immobile, faces that surely could not express emotions such as love and happiness, or even fear. "We sh uld keep ur eyes alert f r them," Soubriquet typed, delighting in his mischief-making. "And we must take care."

"It may be," he wrote, his final sentences, "that Alfred Busi, if his st ry is t be believed, has enc untered bl dily a vestige f ur ancient selves and ne that threatens, if unstemmed, t trap ur c mmunity in a savage past, a past we had th ught we had cl sed ur d rs and fears against an age ag but has c me again t intr duce its nightmares t ur nce dr wsy neighb rh ds."

Indices would have its eighteen hundred entertaining words on the streets by Saturday. He signed off with a salvo of type-writer keys, "S ubriquet," and with the suggestion—written on the manuscript in pencil—that the illustrations should include that photograph of Busi in his bandages, and cavemen sitting round a fire with, preferably, some bones and "Plenty of smoke!" Now all the tipsy journalist needed to do—though it was tempting to let his office colleagues struggle—was to find a neat pen and fill in all the missing letter *o*'s. Soubriquet would then be ready for his bolt-hole and, with any luck, that sporting version of the woman whom he understood to be the timber merchant's unlucky mother. He would be her husband for the night.

Soubriquet drained his glass, closed his fly, gathered Sarky by the scruff to release him on the street for a night of ratting, and headed for the hub of town. Impulse, effort, and reward.

5

TERINA SPOTTED BUSI in the covered arcades lead-
ing to the market hall, with its great arching roof of glass and
ironwork. She recognized his head—it was hard to miss the
bandages—among the usual Saturday throng, but she did not
leave the pastry shop where she was drinking cloudy, minted tea
and studying the pair of shoes she had just bought herself. She
was not keen to talk to her brother-in-law; she was in town to
boulevard around the shops alone and not have any conversations, even with a relative. She'd see him soon enough that night;
she was one of the concert invitees. She'd wear the shoes, and
something elegant but warm. She'd noticed that the breeze had
an edge to it. The hot-air balloon she'd seen earlier was crossing
town at quite a speed.

When Terina spotted Busi for the second time, she felt she
had to leave her tea unfinished, nod her apologies to the owner,
and set off in pursuit. The man was moving awkwardly, swaying like a passenger made unsteady by a pair of heavy cases after
a week at sea—those are not unusual sights in the liner months
from April till October—though his only burdens as far as she
could tell were a copy of *Indices* and one small packet wrapped

in paper from that wretched draper's where ancient women went
to buy their wraps and fripperies. His one free hand was pressed
into his waist as if he were in pain. It looked as if his stomach had
been kicked. Busi's weighty, painful clumsiness was worrying
and could not be ignored. Not by Terina anyway. She was by
nature helpful and solicitous, though strangers might consider
her polite but without warmth. That was only her loneliness at
work. She'd spent too many hours on her own, too many years.
She wanted to be counted as elegant and kind, yet far too often
was considered fine-boned, haughty, and austere.

Once Terina had cleared the shopping crowds and reached
the quieter business precincts, she was close enough to Busi to
call to him by name. But she suspected he would not welcome
being caught in such a limping state. He might prefer to guard
his privacy, his anonymity. Who doesn't want to pass unrecog-
nized when they are out of sorts? So she would not approach
her brother-in-law just yet but would bide her time. She'd simply keep an eye on him from an independent distance. Maybe he
would straighten up and walk more normally once his stomach
cramp or the stitch or his indigestion had abated. Then she could
continue having not-quite-fun, but pleasure anyway, off on her
own again.

There might have been a time when following her irksome
relative would have been an adventure for Terina to enjoy. She'd
seen films—*Naples in Love,* for instance—in which elegant
women pursued handsome and suspicious men through kasbahs
and crowded alleyways, just as she was doing now. Alfred was
a handsome man, she could suppose. Indeed, when she'd first
seen him up on the stage, she'd fallen just a little bit in love with
him, his voice, the thrilling romances he sang about. They might

have been a couple, she had thought. But then her sister came along and was, inexplicably, preferred. Following Alicia's husband might have provided pleasures in the past; she could admit to that. But she could not persuade herself that Saturday to play the movie star too publicly, any more than she could think of Alfred as an older man worth following, for satisfactions of the heart. Hers was more a mission of concern for her sister's widower, a duty, an inheritance, than it was a romance from a film. She was still alarmed after her visit to the villa on the morning of the attack. The home that Alicia had always kept in fine order was not only in disarray and disrepair, but dirty too. Unwashed crockery, unopened post, cobwebs everywhere. And the frass of timber bugs. No wonder there were animals, both in the rooms and in the yard. It had also been a jolt to find her sister's ashes, still in their tawdry presentation coffer and plonked on the piano top as if they were no more momentous than a candlestick or metronome. How could the husband have been so dilatory? Joseph, who was a mystery to her most of the time, an awkward cuckoo in her gainly nest, had been wise with his advice for once: Uncle Alfred ought to hire a housekeeper, he'd said, or move somewhere with fewer rooms and closer to amenities, and that had been the honest truth.

Busi knew that he was being watched, but not by Terina, not yet anyhow. In the arcades and market halls, he had become aware that he was attracting more attention than usual. It had been years since he'd drawn so many stares, although then they'd been complemented by smiles, requests for autographs, and, frequently, bravos. Everyone was pleased to see his face, it seemed. He'd passed a bar one afternoon not far from where he now was walking, hobbling actually, toward the more anonymous neighborhood of businesses and offices, and all the men inside had crowded at the doors and on the terrace to chink their glasses and applaud. Sometimes fans had followed him, not daring to announce themselves but simply wanting to be close to this celebrity. Not once before had he endured such chilly and such weighty stares as he sensed that Saturday in town. These were not the gazes he had sought and valued as *Mister Al*, those shy recognitions that were mostly accompanied by the background mutter of his name. He had then had the pleasurable choice either to take no notice, as a modest man may do, or to turn and repay their smiles with one of his own, like an ordinary citizen whose manners had not been destroyed by fame. These unfamiliar stares that greeted him as he shambled through the town, a clumsy beast, were not exactly hostile yet neither were they warm. How he wished he had a friend, or someone on his arm to make him more invisible. An Alicia, or someone like Alicia. That student neighbor girl, perhaps. She'd held him by the arm, just days before. He hated anonymity. He hated notoriety. He wanted the endorsement of some smiles.

At first, of course, he blamed the chilly attention he was evidently attracting on the awful shape he was in: not only was he still sporting unsightly bandages and dressings, none too clean by now, he was also laboring in pain. That morning's needle had drilled a tunnel into him. Already there was bruising around his midriff and a neural tenderness remitted to his back, to his groin, and down the ligaments of his legs. This is all the *tenderness* I get, he thought. He could no longer regard his body as a virile thing, capable of any strength or speed, or passingly desirable. Rather, he'd become a sack of grimaces and reflexes, of tics and twitches, spasms and convulsions. The more he tried to keep his body balanced and to walk with confidence, the more he felt dysfunctional and odd. So this is what it felt like to be old and, in some way he had not understood just yet, ashamed, though about what he could not say. It can't have been the rabies, surely. This was his second explanation for the chill. Could it be that everybody on the street was frightened that he'd bite them with his frothy mouth? He was the vector now. How had that rumor got about so quickly? The woman with the copy of *Indices*, perhaps, had wagged her tongue in every shop and at every stall she visited: "You'll never guess who was in the surgery, or why." Or the nurse herself had talked? He doubted it; she was not a rattle jaw. Frankly, he was baffled and discomfited, a man put out. He should have gone home straight from the clinic and rested, practiced for the concert, maybe, instead of fooling himself that after the ordeal of the injection he could expect a satisfying saunter in the town.

Then it came to him. Yes, *Indices*. Of course, of course. He was being recognized and treated with this evident unease because of what was printed in the magazine. The drawing of Neanderthals should have flagged a warning. The term itself was a curse: dirty monkey, stupid ape, "You hideous Neanderthal!" The insults were now being pinned on him. What other provocations might the article contain? Busi stopped midstep and opened up the copy he had bought from the vendor in the market hall. He read it where he stood, as best he could, without even hunting for his spectacles. And what he read was dismaying. *Neanderthal* was not the worst of it. He'd been made to look a fool, not only by Soubriquet but also by that dreadful nephew, whose disagreeable opinions had been thoroughly reported and were bound to taint his uncle by association and by blood. Terina had produced a moneyed loudmouth and a fool.

As it happened, Busi was now only a hundred steps away from the bowfronted architect's studio and the estate agency above which Joseph had his town offices. He did not relish the idea but, on the spur of his annoyance with what was published in *Indices*, he felt he ought to seize the opportunity to tell the young man, face-to-face, what he thought about his shotgun talk, his premonitions of a civil war, his evident belief that people should be driven out of town as if they were a pack of dogs. Busi did not generally enjoy a fight. But he would try to hold his nerve. It was his duty to speak up. After all, he and not his nephew was the subject of the article. They could have their argument, but it need not be ill-mannerly. He'd keep it mild. The boy would have to offer his uncle some coffee, or something stronger, once he'd said his piece, and that would give them time to agree to differ, like a household cat and dog. Then Busi could rest there in the offices for a half hour, say, letting matters cool, before making the ten-minute effort of walking to the botanic pastures and his lunch.

In fact, he very soon began to hope his nephew would not be available but would be somewhere else, philatelizing possibly, or staring at his lifeless butterflies or at his stock reports. "Collecting butterflies with his shotgun!" Busi thought. "Collecting payments with his clouting stick." Whatever happened, he was tired and needed to recover in a quiet room on a soft seat. He looked up at the first-floor offices for signs of life or any sounds. With luck, only the secretary would be working on a Saturday. She was a nice young woman, not as cross as she appeared, but not so keen on chatting when there were letters to type, files to organize, and a doting dog at home, waiting to be fed. He'd only have to tell her, "Spare my knees"—his mother's phrase; how time had passed—and she'd encourage him to sit in Joseph's anteroom, probably, in that cracked, leather chair that Pencillon Senior had occupied an age ago. She'd clatter on with what she had to do, ignoring him. Then the offices could be a restful rabbit hole, and an opportunity to regain his physical composure without the fatigues of an argument. He was too angry for an argument. Too old and angry, and too bruised.

Busi turned his back against the far too nosy streets and sighed with some relief as he stepped into the office's entryway. Before he had a chance to pull the bell, he noticed in the window of the estate agency—he could hardly miss it—what surely had to be, but surely not, a photograph of his own home, his villa on the promenade. For the second time that week, his armpits flushed with overwhelming sweat. He went to hot and cold at once. He leaned forward to see the picture better, and caught the mirrored reflection of his sister-in-law in the glass. She was staring at him from the far side of the street, wearing one of her cool summer outfits, its hem vaguely transparent and embroidered with a frieze of stars. He turned to greet her, but she'd stepped back into the entry of a shop, clearly not wanting to be caught. This, again, was baffling. Even Terina was rebuffing him this Saturday.

Once more Busi stared at the photograph of his family villa, while also using the reflection to keep an eye on Terina. She had disappeared for the moment, so Busi pressed his nose against the glass and, without the benefit of his reading spectacles, tried to

find out why his home was on display in the sales window under
Joseph's offices. It was not the only home on show, of course,
but it had prominence. The photograph was a lightly tinted pan-
orama of the seafront residences at the far end of the promenade,
with the Pastry House and then the Busi family home on the
right-hand side, before the ancient shadow of the trees. You
could not tell the ocean was a score of steps away, across the
road, behind the photographer's back, or that the day recorded
on his film was windy and in spring. But Busi knew. He recognized its seasons and its moods.

What was surprising and alarming was how shabby the buildings had become. Busi knew the Pastry House was run down,
but he hadn't realized his own home was in such a flaky state of
disrepair. The photo's monotones and subtle tints revealed those
blemishes that during daylight and in full color melded in invis-
ibility. His villa tilted slightly to the east, and its painted frontages seemed as scaly, peeled, and raised as lichen on a wall. The
high trees of the scarp hung over it like ghastly predators, the
fingers of their branches almost gripping the roof and loosening
the tiles. If any one of those great limbs came down in a gale,
Busi would have timber on his bed. They needed surgery.

Next to the photograph, there was a stylish painted illustration of a row of liner-built apartment houses, their balconies and
prows lined up like some great flotilla, their curved windows bil-
lowing. Busi might not have bothered looking at it if the artist
had not sketched in an almost exact copy of the trees that fin-
gered Busi's own villa as a shadowy background to these new
properties. Now they looked more like looping waves in a Japa-
nese print than foliage. Their pattern was exactly the same as in

the photograph but the color had been enhanced from grayish-green to blue. The caption to the illustration read: OCEANSIDE APARTMENTS AT THE GROVE.

Busi stepped back and gasped with such recoil his body shook. He had to steady himself against the entry doors. He was in shock. His own home and the Pastry House next door had been demolished and replaced, in this plan anyway, by something boisterous and boldly nautical. There was not a straight line to be seen. The many crowded balconies on these oceanside apartments had cocktail tables and matchstick figures dressed in raffia suits and gowns, holding tiny flutes of sparkling wine. The architect behind the drawings had designed a fleet of buildings that was comprised of cabins and decks rather than of rooms, and he had peopled them with socialites pretending to be captains.

Busi knew at once what he was looking at and what the future held for him. This was why the untidy student from next door had said: "It's coming down." Here were plans—advanced plans, by the look of it, beyond repair—to build where Busi lived and where Alicia still lingered in the rooms. Why was it, then, how was it, then, that he knew nothing of this scheme? The current owners of the Pastry House had sold. That much he knew. It must have been taken as a logical certainty by the architect and agencies—on Nephew Joseph's word, no doubt—that Busi would do the same. When asked. If asked. Those stiff, unopened envelopes at home almost certainly contained an offer from the developers, or something yet more menacing: a trap that he'd be helpless to resist.

Busi hunted for his spectacles at last to read the smaller print. To the top right of the architect's drawings, hovering in the sky above the impression of trees, was the company logo and a list of its five partners. The name "J. F. Pencillon" was the fourth one down. Busi wasn't even surprised. This is what he should expect from men like Joseph, men for whom a business opportunity could not be squandered in the name of blood or even in the name of taste. Joseph had claimed to like the Busi home, had found it "charming" even. Now it was clear that all along the boy had been more charmed by the villa's value than he had valued the villa's charm.

Behind the photograph of the old villas and the drawing of the new nautical apartments, not noticeable at first, was a scale model of the whole proposal. It was clever and painstaking. Artistic, actually. Realistic too, though nothing moved, not even the whitecapped waves on the shore. Each of the properties for sale was color-coded according to price and the number of rooms, ranging from the "keenly affordable" gray to the gold. The Grove, it seemed, was not just an oceanside development but a massive one that stretched beyond the scarp behind the villas into what had been the only wildness left in town, the scrubby bosk with its ancient shrubs and trees, its undergrowth, its multitude of untamed animals, its boy. Most of the existing trees, it seemed, were to be felled and used, where possible, as building frames (that was Joseph's role, no doubt: "By appointment, Timber Merchant to the Socialites"), though some were left standing in scalloped fringes as decoration and to provide shade for all the "cottages of character" and family compounds that would be completed, it promised, within two years. "Properties will be released for sale from these offices after 1 September. Early bidding is advised. We expect a pricing structure of between . . ." Again, Busi's body shook with the weight and volume of his gasp. How much? How much? What kind of people could meet expenditure like that? What kind of profits did the developers and his nephew have in mind?

The Grove, according to its scale mock-up, was serviced by a wide, expensively landscaped avenue that led through guarded gates directly into town. The homes and houses were in cul-de-sacs, discreetly private and angled to give each of them an ocean view, though only the larger villas—price band "Gold Plus"— on the higher ground had panoramas. The best seascapes came at a further cost. A more hidden service road encircled all the buildings on the estate. Another narrow, private lane switch-backed down a steep escarpment and passed through some main-tained, token forestry made from painted Foamex, and another security gate. It came out on the promenade at the formal gar-dens in front of what had been Busi's villa.

Busi leaned forward once again and studied where his house stood on the model. *Had stood*, indeed. With such a wealth of detail there before his eyes, with such achieved finality in the architect's mock-up, he wondered for a moment if he had only woken from a coma—some further evidence of rabies, possibly—to find that he had lost six months or so and that his home had already been removed. "It's coming down," she'd said. "It's coming down." His villa now was tall, deck-roofed and balconied. Apartments cruised the seafront, bathed by the sun. The model vehicles parked up on the promenade were either large Panache saloons or they were sports cars, open-topped and exhibitionist.

The model-maker, though, had taken one liberty too many. Only with the most grandiose of poetic licenses can architects expect to civilize the ocean; that's why the ocean has survived. But the pebbles on his ideal beach had been tidied away and carted off. In their place, conjured out of the pages of a fraudulent travel brochure, there was a stretch of straw-yellow sand and a row of umbrella cocktail sticks standing in for multicolored parasols. The future residents, whoever they might be, would never lie awake at night to listen to the stony tumbling of the shore, as Busi had so many times since he was born, as had Alicia for their twenty years and more. He shook his head theatrically, to let the parasols and sand understand how unfitting they would be. He was bewildered and aggrieved, but also startled suddenly: a sign. An image of the putti on their gondola below the fire-borne frieze of printed clouds was, by some angled trickery, reflected in the mirror glass behind the model, though when he moved his head a little, the putti disappeared and the sky was uninhabited. Terina, though, was still reflected there. She was peering out of the shop entrance under the pavement canopy, her neck craned slightly forward like someone half expecting rain despite the protection of the canopy. She was looking down at Busi's back as if she'd been deputed by her son to follow him. The pair of them were acting on some plan to separate the owner from his home, that much was obvious. He couldn't doubt it for a moment. No wonder she had hurried over so sweetly and so readily on the morning he had been attacked. That had been her opportunity to, what? Seduce him, possibly. Certainly, she'd not been dressed for nursing. And she had been more intimate than was normal for a relative of her generation—all that business with his hand upon her lap, all the nearness of her body to his own, the clothes she wore, her devastating scent. Those tender ministrations, those salves and bandages, had been applied with something less than fondness. They had been softeners, unguents, embrocations that would make him sell.

He could at once imagine her persuasive arguments of why he ought to sell the family house: "You've grown out of it, dear Alfred"; "You'll make a pot of money for yourself"; "You should move on, now that you are on your own"; "As you get older, you won't want to cope with stairs like that"; "The place needs fixing, the wind and salt are eating into it"; "It isn't safe up there, so close to the forest"; "Next time it won't be a cat that claws your face, but something nastier. Why don't you sell? I'm sure that Joseph would be keen to help you sell. Your loving nephew has a plan to make you safe and comfortable."

"But I am safe and comfortable," Busi said out loud. His words bounced off the window glass with its slightly concave reflexion of a briefly fattened Terina, still lurking on the far side of the street, her clothes too bright for camouflage. He punched the glass, theatrically—a feint—and turned to challenge her, but in the moment that it took to punch and turn she vanished like a sorceress. He heard only the clipping of her heels, but he'd catch up with her within a day or two. She was his quarry now, and he was hers. It would not be long before those clipping heels were standing at his door. Busi anticipated the thrill of saying no to her, refusing her, denying her. The bosk would not become The Grove, he'd say. Not while he was drawing breath and could withhold a signature.

*

But, in truth, he was not yet equipped or prepared for warfare with Terina and her son. He needed to inform himself; he needed to be armed with facts, with every detail of this sly and surreptitious scheme to separate him from his family home. Once more, he turned and scrutinized the proposed development. If it weren't for the glass, he could and would reach in and flatten all the models with his fist and rip the drawings into shreds. He gave the window a second petulant tap of the knuckles, not quite a punch again. His bandaged hand was painful and best not jarred.

Busi could not bear to stay a moment more. He also knew he could not stomach any lunch. What he needed most was to go home to the villa and make certain it was still standing, that his old and heavy key would have a lock to fit. Afterward, if he could summon the courage, he'd open up those envelopes that had been left unexamined on the kitchen shelf for many weeks. He stepped out of the estate agency's entranceway, not daring to look across the street again, not wanting to be cheered by any hot-air balloon, and hurried off as steadily as he could, away from Terina, away from all the sharp-eyed crowds who had been bruising him with stares—"That's *Mister Al*. There's *Mister Al*. Remember him? He used to sing. He's getting old. Just look at him. What has become of him? What on earth has he been doing to himself?"

6

BUSI CHOSE THE MOST direct of ways between his nephew's offices and the place where he had been born and had lived for more than sixty years. He would not retrace the time-consuming flâneur's route he'd begun to follow after he'd left the clinic that morning, the one that would return him to his villa via the arcades and the avenues, still teeming with their weekend customers, and that rewarded walkers with our town's best distant prospect of the sea. In one of his early songs, "Blue Chartreuse," Busi had likened this "beckoning" half-moon of ocean to a shot of liqueur in the concave of a glass. The drinker held it up against the light and caught the colors of the bay, the chartreuse *verte* of the sea at sunrise in the spring, the chartreuse *jaune* of the sea at autumn dusk, the chartreuse *bleue* of summer noon, when sky and water "dress the same." He'd heard that people sometimes ordered Blue Chartreuse in bars and bistros around the town, only to be told the digestif did not exist except for *Mister Al*, or only to be hoodwinked by a shot of curaçao or even a peg of violet Bacchanal, rich man's meth, which could not reflect the colors of the ocean until the bottle had been completely drained. Then everything could be sea-blue. Then everything was sky.

At least Busi's chosen walk that afternoon would be one easy on the legs. It was almost entirely downhill and passed through the more listless, duller neighborhoods and then the riskier areas above the Mendicant Gardens, known, in a descending order of respectability and an ascending order of penury, as the Shabs and the Shods, where the more insolvent families had homes, and, finally, the Sords, where nobody had anything, except a cough—and lice. He'd not be noticed there, or pointed at. The singer's fans had always been the affluent. But if *anyone* was following him—Terina, that is—she'd be hard-pressed to remain out of sight. These flyblown quarters of the town would want to point and shout at anybody quite as old and fine as her. She would not dare to follow him into these neighborhoods, no matter how slippery she had proved to be. He could not imagine anyone as smart and careful as his sister-in-law ever walking down such alleyways and streets, or risking her thin ankles on the curbs and steps. Her stockings would get splashed. Her dainty shoes could not remain unsoiled.

Nobody was following. *Mister Al* had shaken off his tail, at last, his venal nephew's complicit and conniving mother. Terina, reassured by Busi's sudden burst of speed and the sense of healthy purpose she had seen in his step when he'd finally moved back into the street, would go about her own affairs—but only after she had seen for herself what it was in the display window below Joseph's offices that had caused her brother-in-law to rap the glass so peevishly. Then, as it was a fine day—chartreuse *bleue*—she would walk across to the botanic pastures, see what was new in the orchid and the cycad house perhaps, take her late lunch with an aperitif in the Bristol Pavilions, and then attend that evening's concert, just a little fortified against those well-trodden songs and her brother-in-law's weakness nowadays for sermonizing at the audience. She'd still be home in time for an early night in bed with her tray of weekend treats and with Caruso on the phonograph. She could be Lucia di Lammermoor, loved and dying among the pillows and the shawls. She could sleep, the tragic heroine, and wake, the diva, juvenated by her dreams. It wouldn't matter—she was hardened to it—that the only pillows on her bed were hers.

The once so very famous *Mister Al* was finally alone in town. He had not walked into these parts for many years and was surprised by how quiet and calm they were. Wealth had a clamor of its own, a noisy ostentation, but poverty—or at least the modest indigence that he could see on these unassuming, artless streets— was muted in the day, when people had their affairs to settle or their suppers to chase down. Poverty is mostly raucous after dark, but in the afternoons either it tinkers or it naps. Here the roofs were made of corrugated tin and not a careful herringbone of tiles or slates; the floors were dirt; the walls were half a brick thick; the water came from a common standpipe, against the back frame of a community latrine; the lights were oil or candle wax; pavements, if they were ever any more than hardened clay, were fractured and uneven. Here were packs of dogs and working horses, children with no schooling and no shoes, men and women with no work, windows with no curtains and no glass. Here were alleys far too narrow for the sun. The roof tins baked or lifted in the wind, but in the canyons of the street the weather seemed remote, a variation of the world reserved for other, richer folk. This was so unlike the place we know ourselves, the one described in travel books, the town of cats and cakes, of terraces and balconies, of verandas and container gardens, and of song.

It did not matter in these neighborhoods that the celebrated *Mister Al*, with his shambling walk, his ragged bandages, his heavy, labored breathing, seemed for the moment more like a beggar than our town's most recent luminary from the Avenue of Fame. The few people who passed him in the lanes and alleyways did not reward him with a second glance; though if they had, they might have considered it unusual that this passer-through was carrying a draper's bag and a magazine, both signifiers of a life beyond their own, and that his clothes were too bespoke and laundered for anything but funerals or summonses to stand before a judge.

Busi felt vulnerable, of course, as any of us might in such a part of town, but, most of all, given the events of that tumbling, undermining week, he felt foolish and betrayed and—he could not find the word at first—*overripe*, as though he were rotting on the vine of widowhood, too dry to pick, too dry and far too silvery with mold to be of any value. He used to see men like himself about the town, no longer young but feeble, and nearly always unaccompanied, and wonder at their lack of majesty or, at least, their loss of it. Foolish old men, he would think. They should not parade themselves, but should stay indoors. He never thought he'd be like them, or that the battle of the generations would be one he'd have to fight on both sides, and be defeated twice.

Busi hurried on, head down, one hand thrust inside his jacket pocket, caressing his *Gryphaea*. If he managed not to get lost in the warren, this route should bring him onto the midpoint of the promenade, close to the tank aquarium, where oddities from off the beach or out of nets were brought (and died), in half the time that it would take him on the safer scenic way. From there, he had only to walk for a few minutes with the familiar comfort of the ocean to his right to reach his own front door and the final comfort, surely, of finding it intact.

He checked his watch. In four hours he would be onstage, pretending to be debonair. But first he needed half an hour's nap. He'd stretch out downstairs, on the reading couch in his practice room. He would not have the strength or even the will, he felt, to climb the stairs. The sooner he was insensible the better. His future seemed too complicated and too perilous even to think about until he'd been restored by rest. Once he'd slept and regained his strength, he might be well enough to contemplate the battles that lay ahead with rabies and with speculators and with a town that, thanks to *Indices*, evidently now regarded him as not so much the singer with the dovelike songs but as some old fool who'd grappled in the middle of the night with a naked little girl and tried to shrug it off as an encounter with Neanderthals. Soubriquet—God damn the man—had reported only prurience. What was a tragedy had been dressed up as comedy. Still, at its tragicomic heart, there was a child, there truly was a child, and one that needed saving.

We should not be too surprised that, on what some might consider a foolhardy whim but he maintains to this day was his overwhelming duty, Busi paused at the once grand entrance to the Mendicant Gardens, took deep breaths to strengthen his resolve, and walked inside. There was an off chance, just an off chance, that the boy who'd attacked him at the larder, the boy who should be rescued and redeemed, could be living or surviving there among the other drain urchins, bin divers, and guttersnipes that Nephew Joseph via Soubriquet seemed so bothered by. How the child would be recognized, Busi had no idea. By smell, perhaps. Potato peel. By some sodality of shared experience, the singer's blood beneath his nails? By fellow feeling, if fellow feeling could be found despite their great divide of age, and wealth, and breed? Then, who knows what might happen? At least there'd be some proof in the flesh that Busi's version of what had occurred on that night was the entire truth. The child could be his evidence, and also confirmation that the singer was an openhearted soul, compassionate and giving—morality came at a price—ready even to adopt. *Mister Al*, singer and philanthropist! Busi had a sudden image of his assailant standing washed and scrubbed, clothed and civilized, at the larder door at midnight, calmly grazing on the food within, his crooked finger scooping out a plug of pickles or a bogey of jam, like any teenager might. Like any son. Upstairs in his bed, Busi would hear the tinkling of the Persian bells and know the boy was home at last, and know his *son*—his throat went dry at the word—was safe and saved.

Busi hadn't stepped inside the Mendicant Gardens, he realized, for more than thirty years, not since it had become the unofficial residence of anyone who didn't have a door key or a roof, anybody flattened by misfortune or rattled by calamities. The Gardens were in the meanest part of town, of course, and so not a valued civic amenity or one that the richer people had considered saving or redeveloping, even. Where were the panoramas and the ocean views? Where were the trees? Not in the Gardens, that's for sure. The parts that could claim to be a garden and still sustained a balding snatch of grass and some determined shrubs were unkempt and snagged with litter. The few surviving bushes—knitwoods and laurels are impossible to kill—looked like those in cemeteries on which rag prayers were tied and left to fade by families too rushed. Too rushed to pass an hour with their dead. The musty smell of trees and foliage was edged with excrement, urine, paraffin, and burned wood. Busi had to put his hand up to his nose or else he'd gag. No wonder these Gardens had been known as Potty Park and the Latrine. He should have bought a single cigar for the walk, to freshen the air.

Busi, though, was not unnerved, despite the smell. He was feeling purposeful. There had to be a reason why he had ended up inside the Gardens rather than retracing his steps in the moneyed parts of town, as might have been more sensible. He could stand onstage that very night, with an audience of city notables pinned to their seats in front of him, and make a speech, and make a plea. They'd be ashamed when they compared their bourgeois eagerness to enjoy the world (and possess it) with the singer's evident desire to make the world a better place. They'd all be dressed up in their finery. He must remember to dress down. He'd not remove his bandages.

He'd been that day, intrepidly, alone, to investigate conditions in the Mendicant Gardens, he'd say, not doubting for the moment that he would overcome his fear of public speaking. No, he would strike a valiant note to counterbalance what they might have read that morning in their *Indices*. And what he'd discovered was a disgrace. The very decent people there—he'd spoken to a few—were living in conditions unsuitable for dogs, the sort of squalor in which only rats and pigs would flourish. Yes, Busi recognized his purpose now. All that had happened to him in the week had led him to the Gardens, so that he might become their aging champion. He drew deep breaths and raised his chin to see what he might find, and whom he might discover.

What few sturdy huts there were, were roofed either with corrugated sheets, weighed down against the wind by stolen pavers, or with green timbers from the bosk. The lesser shelters there, mostly makeshift and constructed from cardboard boxes and cargo chests and carpeted with leaves and paperbark, were more like nests than homes. This was a garden inhabited by human rooks.

A rook was sorting through some food scraps with her foot. One of the local greengrocers had tipped his rotting fruit just inside the entrance gate and she was searching through the slime, plunging her hands into the mess in the hope of finding something fleshier and more filling—a nub of fat, perhaps, a bone, the burned skin of a roasted joint—than the orange peel, apple skins, and plum kernels that she had tried so far; swill too black and rotten to pass truly as food. Apart from her, the Gardens seemed unpeopled to Busi, until he ventured farther in and peered into the more exposed of their nests. There were many mendicants asleep, or doing their best to fall asleep in their hard spaces, despite the daylight and such a shortage of room. Many had to slumber sitting up. They must sleep by day because the town had of late—in its paroxysms of alarm about the beggar crisis that Soubriquet alluded to—decided that homeless people should not be allowed to take their rest at night. Constables would come with their long sticks and their flashing lanterns to move the sleepers on. The space was emptied out at dusk, then opened up again at dawn. Who knows what civic logic busied the streets with restless mendicants when all the rest of us were in our beds? No doubt the pending logic would demand an eviction in the daylight hours too. The time would come—I almost witnessed it myself—when a gang of men would arrive with levelers and sledgehammers to reclaim the ground; another gang would come with turf and there would be no trace of this repellent poverty.

Just as Busi had expected and desired, there were many children in the Gardens, either sleeping with a parent or a sibling or a chum, their bodies curled around each other for the warmth and company, or else sleeping alone, uneasy in their solitude, their arms wrapped round themselves, like widowers. What coverings there were, were threadbare, gray with insects, heavy with the grime of living coldly, more like beasts than citizens. He did not think that any of them could prove to be the child that he was looking for, the boy who haunted and troubled him. In his mind's eye and with the decoration that a little time provides, he'd been attacked by something lithe and beautiful, ungarmented—a creature both physical and fabulous. None of these mud larks were either lithe or beautiful; rather, they were sinewy and thin. He did not dare to tread too closely, for fear of waking them, of being caught snooping on their drowsiness, the bowl-eyed barn owl in their rookery. Then at the very least there'd be embarrassment, he thought. Or some cussing. A well-fed affluent man like him—even one who was so evidently wounded, lumbering and disheveled—could not expect to make new friends in places such as this. They wouldn't give a damn that he would make a speech on their behalf that night. They'd look to him for food and cash, and not for his political endorsements. What use was it if he might dedicate a song to them and sing it to the wealthy in their weatherproof marquee? Yet, even though he dare not look too closely, he could see enough of their condition to satisfy himself that his boy would not belong to this community. He sniffed the air. The smell was wrong, an urban smell and not the wilder odor he remembered from the larder door. Was he disappointed or relieved? At least he'd looked. And at least he'd decided on a way to help these indigents. He'd speak and sing for them that very night. Now he hurried back toward the gateway and the street, with purpose in his step.

We have a saying in our town: "Turn your back on Trouble, then feel it tugging at your sleeve." *Mister Al*, indeed, had written a song—called "Valediction"—sort of on the subject, though as usual the lyrics displayed more swagger than Busi had ever done himself. It was a jaundiced celebration of *the fling*, rather than of romance or even love. "Be wary as you steal away," he'd written. "In case she wakes / Beseeches you to stay / 'Til morning breaks / Be silent as you lift your coat / To leave / The slightest noise is all it takes / And Trouble's tugging at your sleeve / And Trouble has you by your sleeve / And Trouble will not let you leave." The music was more spirited than the words, he'd always thought, and that set up a satisfying tension between the light and the dark, between the loving and the cruel.

*

Alicia had not cared for "Valediction" at all, and so, in recent years, her solicitous husband and her even more solicitous widower had not performed it much. But he had hummed the buoyant tune frequently to himself, especially—as now—when he was motivated and enthused as well as still being unaccountably anxious. There were reasons to be wary and to steal away, not wanting to be seen or heard. He was humming it contentedly—this was, for a moment, the best part of his day so far, the closest he had come to happiness—when, for the second time that week, Alfred Busi was attacked.

Once more, he could not say exactly who it was, except—again, again—that they were fierce and dangerous. And male.

Yes, this was certainly a male. An adult human male, and dressed. The texture and the smell could not belong to any other animal. Here was not potato peel but cloth. Here was not the stench of earth and mold and starch, but labor and tobacco. For sure, there were no Persian bells. Yet otherwise this attack was a tidier replay of what had happened at the larder and the bins, eerie and unnerving in its similarities, depressing in its seeming regularity. How many more times that week would Trouble grip him by his sleeves?

Again, this wasn't personal. No one in the Mendicant Gardens was Busi's enemy. Anybody straying there would be fair game. Nor was it new. The poor have always begged and stolen, just to lead a life. An arm simply wrapped itself around the singer's throat and pulled his body back until he was allowed to fall against his assailant's thighs and slide onto the ground. He felt his trousers thicken with the mud. The shame of it, of being wet, of having swampy hands and filthy cuffs, of losing balance and his dignity.

Busi knew he had to stand again. His attacker was too skillful, though, and too experienced to let his quarry arrange itself, let alone resist. He briefly showed the blade—a razor set in a cheap bone handle—with which he'd quite readily slice off Busi's nose and ears and then his prick if he'd not cooperate. Then came another practiced plié and a shove, and Busi's right cheek was pressed into the puddle where he'd briefly sat. The front of his clothes were sodden too. Now the man had got his boot on Busi's back, and he was stooping to empty his victim's pockets. Of course he'd help himself to everything this old man had. Why wouldn't he? Busi must have seemed like a basket of Mr. Klein's stales had seemed to the creatures in the clearings of Poverty Park—easy pickings. The only comforts in such people's lives would come when they helped themselves. This man's gains were meager, though: a fob watch and an ancient key, a pair of spectacles, some loose change and a wallet that contained business cards, a few banknotes (enough to buy, perhaps, an octagon of wine or two bottles of liquor but not enough to make much difference) and a photograph of Alicia, wearing the bouncy blue frock that Busi had always liked. She was holding her shoes above her head, and standing ankle-deep in flood water, in Venice, on a slipway, a joyful, pretty, honeymooning girl. The robber, this enterprising hunter-gatherer, also found the devil's toenail, the singer's talisman and pocket friend for more than fifty years. It wasn't thrown but only tossed. Good Fortune rolled into the scrubby undergrowth, among the litter and the waste. And, for Busi, so did Time. The last few days had passed at speed; the last two minutes had been glacial.

Now Busi heard his copy of *Indices* being shaken out, in case anything had been concealed in its pages—other than the Truth, that is—and being tossed away. The little packet that contained the scarf he'd bought for Terina was snapped out of his hand. He felt his ankles being twisted and his shoes pulled off. Then his face was flipped onto the left and his mouth pulled open. The robber's breath was on his face; his fingers tugged at Busi's lips as if they were as dead as rubber and probed into his mouth. This was mystifying and more painful than anything that day (and this had been an agonizing day already). Later, once he'd worked it out, he thanked his lost Good Fortune in not having any gold teeth to be wrenched from his gums or dug out with the razor blade. Busi wondered if he ought to bite the man, to remove at least his little finger at its joint as a hero would in the cinema, but he dared not. It's always better—excuse the pun—not to take on more than one can chew.

He'd not remember all the details after that. He certainly received some blows about the head, to silence him—he must have screamed—but, mostly, once his mouth had been released, there was little pain other than the pain he'd brought into the Gardens himself: the bruising from that morning's puncturing, the persistent soreness from the boy's attack, the battle scars of age. No one had sunk their teeth into his hand or wrist; no one had latched their claws onto his lips. Nothing would require another plaster or more bandages. Perhaps the fact that his victim was already sporting bandages and wounds across his face and mouth had made the man show pity and exercise restraint. Otherwise his treatment of Busi might have been more brutal. There might have been more blood, more damage to the bones, more muddied dignity.

Despite its bloodlessness, this second attack was worse than what had happened with the boy. It was unnatural, unneighborly, *unkind*, beyond the realm of even beasts. And it was unnervingly anonymous in ways that the boy's attack had not been, faceless though that was. This man had been too competent to show his face even for a moment. All that Busi could be certain of, if he ever overcame the shame and the embarrassment and reported what had happened to the police, was that the mendicant who'd spread-eagled him was fond of his tobacco and slapdash when he wee'd. It would be easier to describe the man's razor and its bone handle than it was to guess the fellow's height or weight or age, or even if he'd ever used the razor on himself and had no beard. No doubt Terina would decide he had been assaulted by another cat. No, this was definitely a human, though from the low end of the species. It was money that had been most desired and hunted for that afternoon, and only humankind wants that. A cat, a dog, a feral boy would have no use for purses tight with notes or pockets full of change. Or even shoes. God knows, they don't want shoes. Or saffron scarves. Or fob watches, spectacles, and keys. They want only their warmth and food, the dull, beastly happiness of full bellies, and a place to rest when they have tired of running free.

There was something Busi would not forget, however, a coda that would haunt him till the day he died. While his head was tipped back and his eyes widened, to allow the robber's fingers to explore his mouth, he saw two pairs of shoes shuffling in the litter and the mud a few paces away. So there were three of them at least, the leader and two henchmen. One pair of shoes was open at the toes and so badly scuffed and thinly laced that Busi understood at once where his own nice shoes were destined to end up and be worn out. The other pair were gleaming new, in patent black, and with the label from the shop still dangling from an eyelet on the lacing throat. During the few seconds that Busi stared at them and wondered at their unseemly cleanliness, their owner lifted up one foot and rubbed the toe cap on the back of his trousers, either to wipe them even shinier or to scratch an insect bite. Then the second of the henchmen stepped forward with a young man's gait and gave Busi quite a gentle kick on the forehead by way of a farewell: *It's over now. You're free to go, old man.*

7

IT WAS LATE AFTERNOON when Busi, stripped of shoes and stripped of all his pocket wealth, reached the front steps of the villa and secured the second, hidden key to his front door from its niche behind the frame. That foresight was Alicia's; she'd been the last to hold the standby key. He closed his fingers where her fingers had once pressed and sensed her warmth, the only warmth that lasts. Thinking of her made him hear her speak, saying he should change the locks, now that the master key was in dishonest hands. And that he ought to change his soaking socks, as well, and not walk the weather round their house. Change everything, in fact. He muttered, "Love you, like a sewer," his reassuring mantra, whenever she surprised him with her unbreathing voice, whenever he was truly sorry for himself.

Who wouldn't feel self-pity on a day like this? It had been a Saturday of shocks and bruises, starting with a puncturing and closing with a drenching. In the final minutes of Busi's unsteady shuffle between the Gardens and the villa, the afternoon had duffeled itself in coarse, thick cloud and then unbuttoned with a heavy show of rain. In this town, we are used to *sudden skies*, as they are called. One moment there is blue chartreuse. The weather dresses us in shorts and shirts. And then, the next, within a pace it seems, the leads, the pewters, and the slates descend as suddenly as death to empty out their buckets on our heads. Then, before we have a chance to shake off the water, the sunshine has returned, sinewy and heavy, and what we might have counted as a mugging by the rain becomes instead a cause of splash-faced happiness. We lick our lips. Their taste is thinly flavorsome.

Busi could not experience that wet-through happiness himself, although he had known it many times in the past and he recognized it now in the grins of the few sheltering pedestrians on the promenade and a couple on their bicycles, delighted by the puddles, and on the face of the cook from the fish restaurant, who, as was the custom, threw a piece of dry bread into the storm, "to soak it up." No one had offered Busi their arm or asked if they could help, although his hurts and incapacities were surely clear to see. All they noticed was yet another ancient down-and-out, and down-and-outs are always slow and shuffling, muddied, blooded, drunk, ill-kempt. He'd be washed and sobered by the rain. What could they do but let him be?

Busi, though, was relieved not to have encountered any neighbors or acquaintances in these final moments of his flight. The loss of light had helped him there, had protected his privacy and concealed from passersby what he had to think of, for the moment, as his shame. His leads and pewters would not go away and let the sunshine in. He'd been robbed of happiness, along with his talisman and the other front door key, and he was old and wise enough to allow his feelings of dismay full vent. He was dirty, soaked, and tired, but there were easy remedies for that. His many cuts and bruises would repair themselves in time, even the latest. The crown of his head was throbbing, twelve beats to the bar. He passed his hand across his temple, wincing at the pain, and felt the clothy square of lifted skin where the man in the Gardens had kicked, so needlessly, with his busted shoe and where the blood had already started to congeal in lacy, puckered scars, despite the rain. His forehead felt as cold as clay. "It's over now," the man had said. But he was mistaken. His kick—unlike the theft—had been unwarranted, undue, and so its bruises would be permanent.

For the moment, if Busi was hoping to find some meager solace in the robbery and beating, this was it; this is what he'd learned between the Gardens and the promenade; this is what that parting kick had implied: his public life had reached its tipping point. Behind him lay celebrity; before him was obscurity. And insignificance, perhaps. Was this the end of *Mister Al*? That was not the worst of prospects—just the logic of the hand that he'd been dealt in life, at birth, which would be trumped when he grew old. That much was always in the cards. The trouble with talent—as with beauty, as surely Terina had found out— was that it was paid in one lump sum, up front. Use it fully, and the day when it will be spent is unavoidable. But, though *Mister Al* might very well be stepping off the stage after that evening's concert in the marquee, the curtain drawn on his last song, *Alfred Busi*, whatever he was feeling on the villa's step, would still have lyrics to perform, without an audience, would still have private melodies.

An ocean breeze had picked up, giving muscle to the tide and setting off a timpani of pebbles on the beach. It rattled for attention at his villa's shutters and window frames. The forest leaves were rustling, a susurrating chorus for the sea. Across the paved square, where vehicles could turn, an entertaining debris squall

made the world seem weightless for a while, picking up and tossing strips of kelp and paper bags and even someone's dislodged
hat as if they were as light as spume. The gale's eccentric detri-
tus left one end of the promenade windswept and the other—
Busi's—wind-strewn. His villa seemed less a place of safety now,
and more a castle under siege, and one—Busi could not deny it
anymore—needing some attention. He stood and looked at it,
the home he'd cared for, and saw it through a different, crueler
lens. It was shabby on the outside, that's for sure, and seemingly
unloved. Not unlike himself. Even the front door, made, before
he was born, from the hardest tarbony—a wood that could survive longer, they said, than a slab of iron—had been so pitted by
the salty wind and a century of stormy seas that it was swelling
and as rough to the touch as the trunk of a living tree.

The long replacement key fitted in the lock with some
resistance—Busi's aging wrists were stiff—and the mechanism
turned unwillingly, defensively, as if it sensed its days were numbered. Even the entrance lobby, in between the street door and
the hall, was gloomy and unwelcoming. For a few moments,
Busi recalled when he was a boy and there would always be a
greeting on his return from school. His mother might cry out, in
her bright but don't-disturb-me way, or else the housemaid, Cla
(he'd never known what that stood for, and—it was shameful—
neither had his parents), would scurry up the corridor, wiping a
glass of cordial with her duster, so that the first sip often tasted of
the oil she used for polishing the furniture. Or else the little ter-
rier they kept would run, busy at both tail and teeth, barking his
demands for attention and wagging with delight. Or else—less
commonly—his father might have come home early from his
offices and he would call out, "Alfred, Alfred, show your face.

Tell me everything about your day. No, tell me *one* thing. Tell me what was best about the day."

And then there'd been Alicia. She never disappointed him or used a don't-disturb-me voice when he came home, as far as he recalled. It didn't matter if he'd been away a month on concert tours or only for an hour in the town, she always kissed her fingertips and pressed them to his mouth, then let him brush her forehead at its hairline with his lips, the not quite kisses of a self-conscious couple still in love but reticent. This little lobby space inside that flaking door, between the bluster of the seafront and the calm of the rooms, was meant only for coats and umbrellas and shoes, but it had witnessed their embraces and reunions a thousand times, and so, for Busi, it had tender memories. They'd guide each other at the waist and step inside the hallway of what had been a never silent house, even if the sounds were only day to day: the hissing of a pan, perhaps, the cracking of logs in the water heater, the flap of curtains, the creaking of the villa's timbers, the tinkling Persian bells, disturbed by someone at the larder door, or simply by the drafts that modern architects abhor but that are the breath of life for homes.

Now, on this catastrophic Saturday, not over yet by far, there was nothing in the lobby by way of greeting, and little in the hallway to welcome him other than the booming weight of widowhood and the fear that he was slowly losing touch with love. For love, like talent and like beauty, is paid in one lump sum and can be spent. It's like a building too: it needs attention and repairs or it will degrade.

There were more than a dozen unopened envelopes on the kitchen shelf. Busi shuffled through them with a shaking hand. What had his nephew suggested just a few days previously at the unveiling of the bust? "Read your letters . . . Stay in touch. And try to answer them." That spurious advice had not made any sense at the time, but now it fitted in. Terina must have spotted the disregarded post when she'd come round that morning, and reported back to her impatient son. Busi, finally, would see what they contained. It wasn't difficult to spot the one he dreaded but expected. It was the most embossed, fat with documents and had the company title on the label. It was addressed—a little oddly—to ALFRED BUSI, RESIDENT. "Dear Mr. Busi," it began. "Forgive us for our forwardness, but . . ." Never had a *but* carried with it so much wheedling and coercion.

Busi had already seen the plans and drawings in the estate agency's window, but how the villa and its current, single occupant would play their parts in this was still a chilling mystery. He had to read the letter twice, grappling with its ornate formulations, before he could identify the offer they were making. As "a valued friend," they could "proffer" him, by way of payment in kind (rather than laying out any cash), "a continuity of residence," in that the three-story, nineteen-apartment building that would replace his own villa and the Pastry House could still provide a home for him. It'd be "a very stately" set of rooms, with ocean views ("just as before") but with the added attraction of "utility support" and "community caretaking." Not only would Mr. Busi be entirely free to choose and fully own any of the apartments that took his fancy, except the uppermost, the penthouse with the garden deck and panoramic views, but also—and here he could almost hear the developers drawing breath with pleasure, as in half a sentence they doubled their enticements—they would put another apartment at his "discreet disposal." He might not own this second one but he could lease it out and take a pension from the rent until the last day of his life. He'd have a milk cow of his own. Their calculation was, he thought, that he'd not live long enough for their seeming generosity to be a long-term business liability. However, he could not pretend that the prospect of both departing and remaining in the way they suggested was entirely without cunning or appeal.

The final flourish of their blandishments was personal and written in blue ink as a postscript to the letter. "Uncle, this is wonderful," it read. "Everything is solved for you. Welcome to The Grove. Your loving Joseph." Busi checked the letterhead, with its list of partners, knowing what he would find. Yes, there it was once more, the surname "Pencillon." He had not expected, though, to see the surname "Klein," and featured twice. Only that morning, in the doctor's treatment room, he had thought about the twins—with some regret—for the first time in many years. Now it was as if he'd summoned them, and put them on the letterhead to make this plot against him and his home appear more sinister and embedded in his past, connected somehow to the clearings in Poverty Park. He blinked, but, no, he hadn't been mistaken. There were the names, "Simon and Gilad Klein," Sigh and Guy. He knew the twins were rich and powerful, and that their shops and restaurants were celebrated for their liveliness and for their civility—they had their father's cakes to thank for that—but he hadn't thought they'd dip their spoons in property. But then, of course, they'd lived next door and clearly had remained the landlords of the Pastry House and were now its unsentimental vendors.

Well, this much was certain. Joseph wouldn't inherit his uncle's cakes. Busi hadn't made a will so far. He'd expected that he'd live and sing for many years to come. But had he died that afternoon, at the toe end of that kicking man at the Mendicant Gardens, everything he loved and owned would legally go to Joseph Pencillon, his one blood tie, and would also benefit Terina. That included the villa, or any oceanside apartment that replaced it. "Welcome to The Grove," indeed! You could not say "Your loving Joseph" was not smart. But Busi would be smarter still. On Monday he would find a lawyer and formalize his affairs—the music at his funeral, the placement of his ashes, the wording on the little brass plate, the special gifts, endowments, and bestowals he would make in death, his archive of notated compositions, the legacy of his home, some provision for a further statue in the Avenue of Fame, his savings and his future royalties to . . . well, not to any Pencillon—though there was nobody more close. He had only the Pencillons. They were now his adversaries, the pair of them. He'd not expected any less from his nephew, though Terina's disloyalty not only to Busi but also to her sister had been dismaying and a jolt. She had been ensnared by Joseph as, he supposed, all mothers were ensnared by sons.

Was this another trick of time, a further trick of age, that parents as they whiten and degrade are happy to inherit from their children? That's to say, their habits and beliefs, not wealth. You inherit first from your own offspring, and then from your grandchildren. And learn from them. They have the wisdom now. The young will do the new things first. They are our predecessors from the future and we have to copy them. Terina, it occurred to him, was copying. She was becoming more like Joseph by the day, beginning to resemble him—that dismissive gesture with his hand, the "Why don't you . . . ?" questions that the pair of them employed, his greed. She was taking after him, instead of the usual and expected opposite that the child becomes a mirror of the parents. No, nowadays she was the child. She surrendered and deferred to Joseph as any loving mother might, doing all she could to be like him, to please him too, even as he did his utmost not to become like her. Well, Busi need not worry on that score. He'd not be ensnared by anyone. He'd not inherit anyone. And nor would they become his heirs.

Busi's gloominess needed shaking off. He walked back along his entrance hall, stepped into the lobby, and opened up the large street door again to return Alicia's spare key to the niche where it belonged—he'd have to get another cut on Monday for himself—and to look out on the now darkening promenade and count his blessings. How lucky he had been to have this lifelong outlook, across the bay, across the ocean, wide and large enough to bow a little, he had always liked to believe, with the earth's colossal curvature. Nobody would ever be able to build on that, despite what could happen to his home or to the bosk where he had played so often as a boy. His town would keep its view, no matter what those letters demanded from him. He leaned against the inside jamb of the door and watched the dimming of the day, the dusk receding to his right, the night arriving to his left. The evening wind, mustering on the promenade, swept away what little heat remained, then made its way across our celebrated bay, its sea whipped up, its waves as stiff and eggy as meringues, to chase away the light. Now there was nothing to be seen, except the blinking of the navigation buoys, the clustered orange lanterns of moored boats, and the white beams of the light tower on Fort Island, drilling at the night. And there was nothing to be heard apart from the tide-loosened chatter of the pebbled shore and the screaming syllables of sonneteering gulls.

Despite the horrors of the day—the horrors of the week, in fact—Busi was no longer as agitated as he'd been when he got home and faced the letters on the kitchen shelf and contemplated what should happen when he died. The letters, actually, had settled him. He'd heard it said that the more disasters a man endures, the less they worry him or make him fret. Rather, they will leave him strong; each misfortune should be welcomed and embraced. And anger was "the harbinger of courage," a productive partnership of spleen and heart, which turns the chick into the fighting cock. Well, Busi thought, he'd had his share of anger and misfortune, so now he could expect a flush of fearlessness and strength. His microphone would have to be a megaphone again. Oh, well. He let out the deepest sigh, and with it half a laugh in recognition of the plight he was in and the decisions he would need to make.

The sighing and the laughter hurt, of course. Busi's ribs and stomach were blackening beneath his muddied, sodden clothes. His feet were aching from the hardships of his shoeless walk home from the Mendicant Gardens. The sudden storm had soaked him to the bone. His face scars had tightened, and they tugged and stung whenever he opened his mouth. He wasn't quite the fighting cock just yet. Nor was he the songbird. With the best will in the world, he couldn't promise anyone a performance to be proud of or even, at the very least, a dignified appearance. He would be handing back his Worthiness Award. No, it was clear that he should and would not turn up at the concert that evening (any more than he could face a second visit to the rabies clinic; these twin decisions seemed linked in some way that he couldn't

yet explain). How could he sing? How could he play? How could
he deliver that noble and heroic speech about the horrors he had
seen that day to all those swells and bigwigs in the marquee and
to the multitude outside, when he could hardly stand without the
doorjamb as support, when he did not much like public speaking
anyway?

It was ignoble to admit it, cowardly, but the beating he'd
received—especially that final valediction of a kick—had made
him feel that those people in the Gardens, ill-fated though they
were, were not entirely worthy of support. Not now. Not ever,
possibly. He need not speak or sing for them. He pushed the villa's
great front door and shut it against the world outside, against the
weather and the night, against a week that would soon end. He
felt himself reduced, as if he'd cut himself in half. Now he truly
was alone. *Mister Al* was left outside, standing in the street, a
recording only, molded shellac, not a life.

Busi retreated to his wide piano stool, his duet stool, which
he had first shared with his mother, learning his chords, then
with his music tutors and instructors, and then with his wife.
She'd slide onto the stool, on his left side, while he was practicing or composing and press her shoulder onto his. She'd never
put her fingers on the keys, except to dust them clean, but she
had sung along if there were words. Now, without switching on
any lights, Busi rested his hand on the coffer containing Alicia's
ashes, seeking her advice. "You ought to telephone," she said
to him, speaking to his palm. He nodded in the darkness. Yes,
of course he ought to phone with his apologies, explaining his
dilemmas, expressing his regrets. This was dreadful, wasn't it?
There could be two hundred people in the ticketed seats expect-

ing him to sing, important people, all of them, and possibly some of his long-term admirers in the gardens beyond the marquee. He ought to phone the concert organizers straightaway, so that cancelation notices could be posted and the more distinguished guests forewarned. Some of them would appreciate an early chance to make other arrangements for their Saturday evening. Perhaps he ought to write a statement they could read or later publish in *The Register*: "Our town's fêted father of the song was too unwell . . ."

But what could he tell them now? That he'd been beaten by the poor and robbed, exactly as his nephew had warned in *Indices*? Or should he say that he was fearful he'd contracted rabies? He had the symptoms after all, and they were getting worse. He'd aged a decade in a week. His body was on fire. They'd understand. They'd have to understand. Or should he rather keep those details to himself and plead that he was too upset by what that showman, Soubriquet, had written in his article? The man had made a fool of him. How could he now perform knowing that the audience would have read that weekend's magazine? The word *Neanderthal* would be on everybody's lips. Or should he claim (for it was partly true) that the wounds across his own upper lip and on his wrist and hand would hardly let him sing or play convincingly? They will have read the news report in *The Register* and seen the photograph, even if they hadn't yet bought *Indices*, and so would be aware that he was wounded. Or should he put the blame at Joseph's feet, at Terina's too? They—the wealthy in the town as well, the businessmen and estate agents in the audience—had let him down with their grand and selfish plans. He'd not perform for them. It was a matter of principle that he stayed away. His absence from the microphone could be, he'd say, his rejection of The Grove.

All of these excuses contained their grains of truth, of course, for Busi was an honest man. But, despite the urgency—by now his guests and fans would be pulling on their coats and shoes—he could not bring himself to lift the receiver from the telephone. None of his explanations, the singer knew, was sufficient to do what he had never done before: fail to honor a concert booking, fail to show up on the stage. He'd performed, outdoors, in thunderstorms, and with a fractured ankle, with malaria, with migraine, with diarrhea, on the day his mother had had a stroke, the day he'd crashed into a horse-drawn cart (the horse had had to be put down, but Busi sang), even on the evening after Alicia's death, because he'd given his word some months before and he was professional. He turned up early and he stayed the course, no matter what. He'd persevered when there'd been floods and riots in the streets around the concert halls, in power failures. (Singing in the dark with no amplification had been both a complication and an unexpected joy.) He'd plowed on through his repertoire, even with those audiences who were either bored or hostile, or coughing uncontrollably. He even carried on—in Bellagio—when he'd been told, before the start, that the venue had gone bust; he'd not be recompensed. His hotel bill would not be settled either. "The audience have paid, so I shall sing," he'd said unselfishly—although he'd not resisted the temptation to announce to satisfying applause after his first number what he had done for them: "I'm more than compensated by your kind ovations and by the beauties of your lake."

So it was not an insignificant decision for Busi not to show up at that evening's concert, especially if, as now seemed most likely given his evasiveness, he'd not even let them know beforehand and offer his excuses. They were too lame and insufficient. Each of them would make him feel an even bigger fool. Could he say the honest truth, the greatest truth—and this was something surely they would understand—that the yolk had gone out of his egg since Alicia had died? He'd done his best to carry on. But, actually, his widowhood had flattened him. It might have taken him two years to recognize the truth, but his wife had carried off his songs. His appetite for performing had been cremated with her bones. Again, he put his hand onto her ashes, and for the second time that day said "Like a sewer" to his wife. But, no, he could not share this with them either. Indeed, he was suspecting he'd prefer that his absence was a mystery. Let them gather; let them miss him and his songs; let them wonder what had happened to their *Mister Al*.

Busi curled and folded his arms onto the keyboard lid and used them as a pillow for his damaged head. He was appalled to be so cowardly and weak. A better, prouder man, he thought, a more courageous, operatic man might take a knife and cut his throat, or search in the medicine cabinet for pills, or in the outhouse for some pesticide, rather than face the indignities that lay ahead. Maybe it was just as well that he'd never taken Joseph's advice and bought himself a shotgun, because it would be too easy for the singer to blast all his problems to smithereens. There'd be no need for explanations then. They'd find his body in the villa, he imagined, in a month or so, too decayed and maggoty to recognize. Half eaten, probably. Those bin diners would battle through to him, attracted by the smell. For a moment, he imagined the boy—his boy—kneeling at the side of his corpse, then ducking down to plunge his teeth again into the daintiest cuts of meat, Busi's cheeks and lips.

Busi would not kill himself, of course, and not only because he did not want his house and wealth to go to any Pencillons. And not because the only pills he possessed he'd already taken for his headache on the night of the attack. And not because the only weapon he had was that gentler one, his father's walking stick, which so far as he knew had only ever drawn the blood of Simon Klein. Even if he had the dexterity and strength to knock himself unconscious with that stick or, even, to douse himself in something flammable and set himself alight—Alicia's Boulevard Liqueur might do the trick; its flame was green—he would not do so, not because he was too cowardly but more because the only gestures he employed were on the concert podium. In life, he was not theatrical. Suicide was stagy, overdone. It was embarrassing and cheap, suited to the *Al*s but not the Alfreds of this world.

*

Alfred Busi fell asleep sitting on his practice stool but not so deeply as to evade his nightmares or his dreams. He was disturbed frequently, though briefly, whenever he shifted his arms or his head on the hard piano lid, and once by his telephone ringing. He knew he ought to answer it, then find a bed or a couch or even curl up on the rug beneath his feet, but he could hardly summon the energy before he dozed again. He relived the Garden beatings in his semistupor; he revisited the day when Papa had been bitten by the bat; he lost himself in a maze of alleyways and insults, of funerals and storms; he felt his mother's fingers on his face and then the stinging of the salve; he whirled his clouting stick around his head and went for strangers in the street; and he went for Joseph Pencillon. His slumbers were exhausting and unkind.

Unusually for him, Busi would remember his dreams, or at least a muddled portion of them, when, after more than an hour, he woke and lifted his head from the piano. He would remember either going to the marquee in the town hall gardens and singing for the audience, or not showing up at all, and no one missing him. He would remember booing *and* applause. He would remember the distant cracking and the smell that interrupted his first piece and caused his admirers and his fans to shift with worry in their seats. It's just the static from the microphone, he'd said, unconscious as a stone; it's just the cables burning with the ardor of my songs. But he knew, he'd always known, this final Saturday should be engulfed in flames, and so he made it happen in his dreams.

During that more than an hour of uneasy sleep on his piano stool, Alfred Busi, pluckier than life, had walked out into the villa's yard, pushing aside the refuse bins. Maybe he had toppled them; perhaps a pair of cats had arched at his passing and spat their curses at him. For the first time in more than fifty years and only in his slumbers, he began to climb the loose limestone scree on the steep embankment of the bosk. At one moment he was naked; at another he was shoeless, bruised, and old; and at another he was just a boy, little Alfred Busi living an adventure while his parents slept. It was nighttime, it was daytime, it was spring and there was blossom on the trees, then there was a nipping wind and spray, and afterward a light that might have been the moon or might have been the sun or might have been the lanterns of the constables hunting with their truncheons for the sleeping poor.

By the time he'd located the well-worn game trail used by the diners at the bins, the wild and ancient woods behind the villa had begun to flatten out. Alfred, Signor Busi, *Mister Al*, the Chanson Dove, whoever he might be in that fragmented dream, was already ripped and torn and bruised; his clothes were shredded and his feet were lacerated by the sharp-edged rocks. The seathorn and the pine scrub had replicated all the abject damage done to him that week, the scratching and the beatings and the puncturings. But these wounds now, up among the trees, were noble ones, delivered by a living world that never meant him any harm.

It might seen ungrateful, then, that Busi, in the thickets of his sleep, had taken matches from his pocket and had already offered just a little warmth and light to this cold scene. He certainly intended harm. He had reached the center of what would be his nephew's "Grove," the unworked timber of the villas and the dwellings they would build. From a distance he could hear his own voice singing in a marquee for the rich and eminent. He could even hear applause. The match's flame guttered in his palm. It had almost burned down to his fingers, so, without a thought, he let it go. The afternoon's rain made the ember slow to catch. But when the box of matches, still nearly full, was dropped and given to that struggling flame, there was a detonation and a puff of sulfur. The bolstered flame caught on the carpet of paperbark and flared. No one had to kneel and blow. The bosk embraced the heat and gathered round. There was a sound like cardboard tearing as the fire expanded and reached out, hunting for marquees.

Busi wasn't really sleeping anymore. The dream was strident with the splintering of burning trees and had half woken him. But he did not want to end it yet. He nurtured it as he revived and let the ancient forests of our town exact their punishments on us. It didn't take much effort to imagine what might occur if fire had taken charge. He had only to close his eyes again and press his face into the pillow of his arms to witness for himself the trouble he could cause with just a match. His guests inside the marquee would have no idea that anything was wrong, but those outside—the ones too poor to pay, too ordinary to be invited— would be bound to recognize the acrid odor of the smoke and the percussion of cracking wood coming from the east side of the town, descending from the bosk. They would see the russet glow on the skyline and know. It wasn't dawn. It wasn't even midnight yet.

Of course, somebody would shout out "Fire"—that thrill is irresistible—and loud enough to be heard inside the marquee, where *Mister Al* either was or wasn't up on the stage. It is always best to step outside if there's a fire, so people stood, in Busi's waking dream, and started filing out, mid-song maybe, not in a panic but not patiently either. Not for the first time that evening there was shoving. The guests were treading on one another's heels. Stockings would be laddered. Coats would be abandoned on the backs of seats.

Joseph would have been the first to leave, in Busi's vision for that Saturday. He'd only have to walk across the empty space between the stage and the front row of seats to find the exit vent that led into the gardens. By the time he got outside, most of the panic would have passed. There *was* a fire but not one close enough to matter much as yet. It was more spectacle than danger and hardly consequential—except that it was always sad to witness forest burning down. Joseph would think otherwise, of course. The *boy*, brought up on money made from killing trees, was not defeated easily. He would see and understand at once. The woods where he and his collaborators—the Pencillons and Kleins—hoped to build The Grove were up in flames. So what? The resin in the carobs and the tarbonies that flourished there and all the desiccated matter in the scrub and undergrowth did not require instruction on how to catch alight or how to burn. A careless cigarette could have started it. Somebody walking with an oil lamp. Someone with a barbecue. Joseph might have started it himself, if he'd have thought of it. It would not occur to anyone, not then or since, that clearing all the trees so speedily and economically, that stripping back the land and ridding it of foliage, was not a tragedy for those who had grand building schemes. Nature's labor comes for free. The town's surviving forest would either have to burn that evening or, in time, be felled. Who doesn't much prefer the drama of a late-night fire to the endless daytime whirr and drone of saws? Not Joseph Pencillon. No, in Uncle Alfred's conscious dream—though more a nightmare now—his nephew's head was thrown back and he was laughing at this fiery stroke of luck.

Busi had to redirect his dream, reclaim it for himself. He had meant to thwart the building of The Grove, not hasten it. He could not have his nephew triumphing again, and saving money too. Nor—he realized too late—could he abandon all the animals that once had eaten in his yard and now would be destroyed by the inferno he had started. He could not let them fry or choke. He had to be their Noah and lead them to their Promised Land, not over waves but through the flames, and westward into town.

According to this closing dream, the specifics of which he only retained in such great detail because within less than an hour he would be retelling it, improving it, for an unexpected visitor, those creatures that had made their homes and livings in and underneath the trees did not begin to reach the safety of the paved and fireproof streets and alleyways until the concertgoers had gone home or, elated by the music they had heard and the dramas they had witnessed before and after *Mister Al*'s perfor- mance (if, indeed, the famous singer had shown up), had found their corners in a bar. The forest birds were first. Great scarves of starlings, rooks, and sparrows. A flame will seldom catch a bird. And then the bats. And then the larger animals, the silver deer, the native cats, the dogs and foxes, and the wilding pigs. For once, the creatures and the beasts had scatty jurisdiction of our town. They could do exactly what they chose. There were too many to be stopped. The streets were boisterous and rowdy in ways unknown to humankind. It was a cartoon film from Hollywood: some fool had failed to lock the zoo and there were startled mobs of liberated animals, baffled by the straight lines and the lights.

Motorists out late and taxi drivers had to brake, then wipe their eyes in disbelief. They'd not seen wildlife on the streets before, except perhaps the squads of rats that lived among us all the time, and cats. One cabby was so flustered and alarmed by the midnight flocks of buntings coming at him through the smoke that he put on his windscreen wipers. Another had to park and wait because the way ahead was clogged up by orders, taxonomic ranks even lower than himself. Another, just avoiding by a fingerbreadth a creature he would describe as something most resembling a naked child but running like the wind as no child ever could, was shamed when he braked to see his passengers slide forward on their seats and end up sitting on the ashtray of his floor. A family of hungry, maddened boars blundered through an open door into a restaurant, attracted by the smell of pork and then alarmed by falling plates and cutlery as diners clambered onto the tabletops for safety. A pair of scrub cats settled down behind the putti in the cushioned hollows of the hot-air balloon's gondola. A badger, baffled by the thickly woven dance carpet on a hotel lawn, failed to dig a hole but did not fail to make a mess.

By the time the smaller beasts arrived, and with them other refugees too rare to be recognized or named (the teeming mass of living things, from snakes and beetles to fleas and flets, who had no love of fire), nearly all of us were in our beds with no idea the town was hardly resting but alive with feather, fur, and hide, and some potato peel. Once the taxis and their final fares had settled for the night, the only creatures on the streets with clothes were mendicants who had been banished from their camps and were already used to sharing what they had with other living things. Away from streets and at the forest edge, the teams of firemen and their volunteers mostly let the conflagration go about its business, burning out until there was no timber left for fuel. They played their hoses on the edges of the fires and let the hydrants freely empty out. There were no humans to be saved, they thought, so why risk any firemen's lives? Just give it time and it will run its course. Let Nature put an end to it.

They were wise to be so patient. Busi's dream was dying

back. At first, his envisioned sky had been dancing high to the flames and was briefly bright enough to paste the ocean with its oranges and golds. But very soon, such was the poverty of the rocky terrain, so thin and weak the undergrowth, so thin and weak the dream, the flames ducked down into themselves, grew hesitant and shrank. By the morning there would be little left but palls of smoke and blackened trunks, although the houses nearest to the fire would be pocked and soiled by heat and heavy clouds of ash. The rain—there had to be some rain—would be heavy when it came, and it would be purposeful, content to have a proper job to do, to wash our windows, clean our motorcars, sweep our streets, sluice our drains and culverts, and put an end to all the drama of the night, the nightmares and the reveries. That's why we sleep. Why would we not? Our town has dreamed much worse than that and not lost any rest.

This was where the maestro of the dream sat up at last and rubbed his eyes. The buttons on the piano stool had left their throbbing imprints on the backs of his legs. His neck and shoulders were so stiff from the contorted way he'd had to sleep that he could hardly stand at first. He certainly could not straighten yet. So Busi hunched his way toward the door and for the first time that evening threw up the switch to fill the room with light. He checked his watch. The concert had begun—and ended, he presumed—without him. Again, his armpits flushed with sweat. His chance had passed. He'd been a coward and a fool not to phone with his apologies, but neither a coward nor a fool not to perform that night. He was too frail and unbeguiling. No doubt of that. But what would happen now? He was sure that either Joseph or Terina would be banging on the villa door quite soon.

They might both come, to press their double blandishments on him. Well, he would leave them on the steps. They could knock the whole night long and still not get an answer out of him.

Busi wasn't hungry but he certainly was cold. He needed to be fortified, so he opened up the larder door and took out what was left of the Boulevard Liqueur and one of the delicate green glasses that Alicia preferred for her wines and spirits. A little alcohol might ease his pains and reinforce his courage. He was pouring out a decent shot, when someone, something, started banging on the kitchen door, not five paces away from where he was sitting. It couldn't be the Pencillons, he thought. The yard gate was bolted against outsiders and he could not imagine Joseph or Terina scaling his high fence. Anyway, it was not like the knocking of a visitor, politely hesitant, wanting to be heard but not wishing to disturb. His second thought was that his boy had finally returned, calmer now. Everything would be resolved. His third thought was that, no matter who the banger on the door might be, he shouldn't answer it, not without his cudgel, anyway. Perhaps, the robbers from the Gardens had come to finish off the job. They had his key, but the front door was too well lit and public. For sure, they wouldn't balk at gaining entry to his yard. His cudgel, though, was upstairs, tucked away again behind the bedroom door. Rather than collect it and reveal himself, he stood as still as a heron, almost invisible in the shadow of the kitchen. Whoever or whatever it might be would go away if there was no reply.

When the banging was repeated, Busi crouched as low as he could, given the bruising around his midriff, and backed away out of the kitchen. He fled silently upstairs to the window in his bedroom, from which he could look down onto the rubbish bins and into the shared yard. He expected mendicants. But actually there was a woman at his door. He could not see her face, but he could tell from her unruly hair and eccentric clothes that this was the student from next door—she'd only had to cross the yard from the Pastry House—the one who'd said, "It's coming down," without a thought about the shock she'd caused, the one who'd asked so brusquely in the street, "What have *you* been doing to yourself?"

8

TERINA HAD ARRIVED ahead of time at the gardens where the concert would be held. She'd come straight from the Bristol Pavilions, slightly tipsy and not in a patient mood. Her taxi driver watched her cross the street in the afternoon's last sunlight and disappear behind the shrubs and statues of the Avenue of Fame before he drove away. Her perfume lingered for a while, as did the image of her from behind. Terina always knew when she was being watched. The scrutiny that she occasioned was of a different kind to that which Busi had enjoyed and endured for many years. His had been the scrutiny of recognition; hers was the stranger's eye, both men and women, looking at her figure and her clothes, and wondering. She was a passing spectacle, defying age. She understood why Joseph might think otherwise, however. She had been an embarrassment since his teens. For Terina—as with many women—it was dressing, not undressing, that was her act of seduction, and so for her son her clothes had been discomforting. For Joseph to see his mother dressed up for the day was just as shaming as the one occasion when he had caught her without a stitch, as straight and thin and featureless, to his eyes, as a broom stale. "No one is looking at you, Mother," he had told her recently. "You like to think you're noticed, but you're not." Joseph, however, was only fooling himself—and leaving his mother ill at ease.

Sometimes it was a burden, to be watched with such intensity. Her body stiffened. She could hardly walk unconsciously. But mostly she was glad to be observed and did not really care whether she was judged to be an older woman turned out well or considered as false and as manufactured as a paper rose. She was endorsed by being stared at, validated, and approved. So she took her time—her new shoes were too stiff for hurrying, anyway—as she proceeded down the line of honored citizens in bronze, reading—often for the first time—the brief citations underneath the many busts: the scientist, the engineer, the general, the man who'd been ambassador in Washington and Rome, the editor, the mayor, the chef.

There was not a single woman in the line. She could not imagine ever being cast in bronze herself or sitting on a plinth until—quite soon—her haircut was no longer fashionable and her dress had aged into a costume. What had she done with her decades except produce a single child, except be kindly when she could? Joseph, though, her distant and infuriating son, might very well command a plinth in years to come, JOSEPH PENCIL-LON, the timber man, the housing developer, the city's richest-ever mayor. Joseph had already said—when they had passed an empty bay in the Avenue of Fame on the day of Uncle Alfred's inauguration—that the space was set aside for him. It was as if our town would recognize only the fame and talent of the men, no matter how unprincipled they were, and the women were like her, wives or mothers or just passing spectacles, strangers to be scrutinized and wondered at but little more.

When Terina reached the singer's bust, still shiny new and not as yet defiled by patina, though roosting birds had done their best to bandage his skull in white, she did not pause to look at it. It was more noble than the man. The sculptor had rejuvenated him, made him seem carefree, when her brother-in-law, in her experience, was nearly always overwhelmed by cares. She could not forget the sight of him that afternoon, how limp he'd seemed and slow, how great the effort was for him to cope with any steps or even scale the lowest curb, how he had seemed to be in pain, how he had been so strangely petulant and then so oddly energized when he rapped his knuckles against the window glass beneath Joseph's offices. It had been a shock for her, when she went forward to inspect the window display herself, to see what had unnerved Alfred. It would have unnerved her too.

She'd studied the drawings for The Grove in the office window with a shaking head. She'd even rapped the glass herself, with her bony hand. That schemer of a son of hers, that little tuck-away of secrets, had private plans—at least, private from his mother—to make a profit out of that dear house that Alicia had loved so much and that her widower had said quite forcibly he did not want to leave. She blushed to think how often she herself had thought that Alfred might be, well, not happier exactly, but easier to manage if he sold up and found himself a smaller, smarter place. Somewhere with fewer rooms and closer to amenities, as Joseph had suggested. But she had never meant to embezzle his emotional assets as her son clearly meant to do. And she had never thought a Pencillon would be involved. How much Alfred had known about all this she could only guess, but she could not imagine that he would ever want to be a player on that stage, although . . .

... although, as Joseph had often said, sounding like his father, "Money is the tune that everybody whistles to." Well, she would face up to her son that night and demand his explanations—and apologies. People might not notice her, in his reproachful view, but they would hear her when she spoke her mind. They both had seats at Busi's concert and neither of them should be fuming while Alfred sang. He would be able to see them from the stage and he would sense if there was any kind of tension. No, she would wait until the entertainment had been concluded and they had both offered their bravos to *Mister Al*, and then she'd take Joseph to his empty bay in the Avenue of Fame and ask him what he had been thinking of with this vain scheme to make homeless his own kith and kin. "You'll not be getting a plinth in here, if you continue to behave like that," she'd say. "And there's another thing. That interview you gave to *Indices*. You really ought to be ashamed. They made a fool of you." She nodded her head as she rehearsed his dressing-down. Her son. Her child. She loved him, but she did not like his principles, but then she could say the same about Pencillon Senior. She'd not married him for principles but because he'd treated her as if she were a queen deserving of the very best, and could afford to do so. And he adored her, in his gruff, pragmatic way. Still, she had never understood why—given the choice—Joseph had so aspired to resemble the father who'd played no part in his upbringing and not resemble her at all. This time she shook her head from side to side, and blew out air. "Let's get it over with," she thought.

Now Terina was aware that she was being looked at by a couple of concertgoers following behind, and on this occasion clearly not because they found her elegant or trim. Not only had her head seemed loose, she'd shaken it so much, she also had been talking to herself and tensing her arms, like someone trying to shrug off restraints. She had been careless to display so publicly the exasperation and the stress of having Joseph for a son. She blushed, offered them a little nod of greeting—not mad at all—and hurried on as quickly as her shoes would allow until she reached the Parting of the Ways.

*

The garden that led to the concert marquee had been divided into two on gender grounds—as public toilets were. The women went to the left and took the Ladies' Walk, past pink and salmon roses. Their husbands and their male escorts went to the right— the Gentlemen's Walk—between the lavenders and blue fessandra shrubs. It was a separation of only fifty paces but quite romantic in a way. The couples had to part or else invite bad luck. "Break the Rule and Break Her Heart" is what they said. The man would let her hand withdraw and watch the woman disappear behind the foliage before proceeding himself on his companionless path. It was not unusual if he ran, to be the first, to be there waiting when she came. Then their hands could join again or they could act out a routine of extravagant greetings as if they had been parted for a year. Terina heard the couple who had been watching her bid each other operatic farewells, and then the crunch of gravel as the woman drew a little closer to Terina. Clearly she was keen to speak.

"I like your shoes," she said at last, although she meant, "Are you okay? You seemed upset."

Terina smiled. "They're new," she said. "A bit too tight," as if their tightness might explain her unsteady head, her tense arms, and her tipsiness.

"They suit you, though. They'll soften up."

The woman seemed less anxious now that she'd heard Terina speak and dared to look her up and down, all the better to admire the thin but tailored dress, embroidered at the hem with stars. Embroidery was fine, Terina thought, so long as it was not too highly colored or overwrought and kept to hems and lapels. But, unlike the woman standing there in front of her, she would not risk materials with patterns. They were for the young. This woman needed some advice. Patterns, tartans, paisleys, checks, anything too busy, make a woman dumpy, if she isn't thin. Cloths and fabrics should be plain; their hues and tints must not be rainbows but unmixed and singular, sober and judicious. She favored clear-skied materials in blue or nighttime black over cheery colors. Terina smiled, and tried to hide the condescension she was too often guilty of where clothing was concerned. The other woman's condescension, though, was not so well disguised, though it was puzzling at first. She overtook Terina with a brisk "Good Evening" and completed the last ten paces of the Ladies' Walk with almost a sprint. Her husband was already waiting there, his arms spread out, his lips prepared. His wife's embroidery and patterns did not bother him. Terina walked on steadily with no one to embrace or kiss, her rage increasing with each step.

The marquee in the gardens near the town hall was made from orange canvas and beflagged, with lanterns hanging from the guys and paper streamers tied to every pole. It was a merry sight, inside and out. Terina was among the first to sit. A place had been reserved in the front row, below the microphone stand and piano that was, at that moment, being tuned after the disturbance of its lifting by a dozen men onto the wooden stage. She never liked these periods of sitting on her own, but she could not bring herself to hope that Joseph would show up early for a change. He was the sort who thought it manly to be late, to still be standing and on show when everybody else was settled in their seats. In that regard, if only that, he had learned something from his mother.

Terina practiced breathing steadily. Those last moments in the gardens, where the genders met, had been humiliating. Every widow had to walk between the roses on her own and not be greeted at the other end, and not be taken by her hand, or kissed, or hugged. No wonder that patterned wife who had admired her shoes had been so happy with herself. She'd no idea what being on your own amounted to. Terina had to shine a bright face at the world or else she would appear sour to anyone that spotted her. Sourness was just as bad as patterns, in her view. Perhaps that's why, when Soubriquet arrived, in his alarming Jimmy Cagney suit, and made his way with obvious purpose through the milling audience toward her seat, she greeted him with her most winning smile, the one in which she showed only her upper teeth between very slightly parted lips. She knew better than to risk her fillings or receding gums.

Terina did not recognize the man, although she knew his face. He seemed a little intimate with her, even taking her hand and kissing it, making up (for anybody watching) for what she'd been denied at the end of the Ladies' Walk. She reeled back through the past few days, trying to place where they had met.

It didn't help when he said his name, "Soubriquet"; she knew the word, her French had once been good, and wondered why this stranger would refer, with such an arcane term, to chucking women underneath the chin. *Sous briquet; sous le menton.* She tilted her head a little and smiled again, trying not to show she was perplexed. But tilting her head seemed to jog her memory. Now she recalled, and just in time, exactly where they'd met— well, *hadn't* met; they hadn't spoken at the time—and made connections quickly after that. He'd been at the ceremony when Alfred was inaugurated into the Avenue of Fame. She'd seen them talking intensely, and at the time had wondered what her brother-in-law might have said that was worth noting down. So this untidy fellow with cat hairs on his sleeves was the journalist from *Indices* who'd made such a fool of Joseph in that week's issue, letting him boil off his steam so publicly. She did not know if she should feel annoyed with him. She could not blame the man for what her son believed. You can't put words in other people's mouths, and she supposed he hadn't made them up. Joseph's voice was grinning through too convincingly for that. She would not complain about the article, therefore, but let the matter rest. Besides, she should be glad that no matter who this awkward stranger was, she was no longer sitting in her seat with no one to keep her company and greet her smile with an amused one of his own. And so—what was she thinking of?—she put up her other hand for him to kiss. And he would have taken it—the woman, in his view, was all the better for this second, close inspection and he would like to smell her skin again—if Trader Pencillon had not arrived and intervened.

Her son had not exactly hit the man, but he had shoved him firmly in the chest and shouldered him away. "Don't even touch my mother," he had said, as if he felt her honor needed saving, though he must have realized by now that it was his own honor that had been traduced in *Indices*. "What is it you want from her?"

"I am being charming." Once more, that very mordant smile. This Soubriquet, though in his fifties, was taller than her son, and heavier.

"Step away. She isn't charmed." The men squared up again and jabbed their fingers at each other's chests, like boys in the schoolyard. "My mother truly isn't in the least amused by this," Joseph said, taking only a half step back and attempting to brush off the inky imprints on his shirt.

That much was true. Terina was not amused by either of the men. If only both of them would move away, she might be able to recover her composure. For no good reason, it concerned her more than anything that the patterned wife was witnessing the contretemps and would have a second cause to feel superior. She was aware that half the conversations in the marquee had stopped mid-sentence, as concertgoers waited for a proper fight to start or greater insults to be exchanged. Finger prodding usually led to something more dramatic. But Joseph sensed he'd get the worst of it, and backed off again. Next time, he'd arm himself with something hard and sharp—his keys, perhaps. Now that there was some distance between the two men, Soubriquet made a show of being nothing but bored and sauntered off, hands in his pockets, his tongue on show, sardonically, in the corner of his mouth. He looked back just once, to incline his head toward Terina. She only hoped that word of what had almost happened did not get back to Alfred in his dressing room.

"How are you, Mother?" Joseph asked, once the journalist

had reached his seat. But she turned her head away and would not speak. She could hardly bring herself to look at him.

If he registered her anger, it did not bother him. He had come in company: two other businessmen she recognized by sight and their reluctant wives and two older men, the Klein twins, owners of the Klein arcade and several restaurants, were sitting in a row to Joseph's right. She was not introduced to them and she was glad of that. She was impatient for the concert to begin, wanted to get it over with, actually, and then survive that confrontation with her son. Terina did not like an argument any more than Alfred did. Was that their age? Her face, she thought, looked pinched and foolish rather than commanding when she was annoyed. On those rare occasions when she had found the nerve to speak her mind, she had upset herself more than the person spoken to or, in this case, not spoken to. Nevertheless, it was her duty to speak up. She was a mother, after all, and it was right that she should caution Joseph when his *plans* engulfed dear members of her and his own family, both the living and the dead, or when he shamed himself in print, or when he made a public display of his short temper. So first the concert—let Alfred enthrall—then, after him, a frank exchange of views. She turned toward the raised platform, keen for the marquee to fall quiet and then applaud when *Mister Al* appeared onstage. The celebrated *Mister Al*.

The hubbub in the marquee was increasing rather than abating, as conversations lengthened and amplified with every minute that the concert was delayed. Guests who had been sitting down expectantly became bored with staring at a platform and the gaping lid of a grand piano and stood up to smoke or look around and wave at anyone they recognized. A group of younger men shuffled past the line of knees where they were sitting and leaned against the performance platform, where they could see and be seen by any woman worth a second look. The crowds outside—the uninvited and the ticketless—pushed up close to the venting in the marquee to peer inside for any clue as to why *Mister Al* had not begun his routine yet.

When twenty minutes had gone by, somebody on the outside started catcalling, and that was picked up on very soon by some of the minor dignitaries inside the tent, who were not used to being made to wait. The more polite among the audience or those who had never mastered whistling began to applaud, sarcastically but infectiously. Soon the marquee space was throbbing with a slow handclap and the growing crowds in the darkened open air joined in, more raucously. Children must have stirred in bed, far off, and wondered what the clamor was. Anybody in the streets as far away as the promenade might have marveled at the hullabaloo on the hill and wondered if they'd missed a riot or a football match. If Busi had gone outside to his yard and bins, instead of sleeping on his stool, he would have heard the din himself.

Finally the marquee manager for that evening, a man who blushed and stuttered under stress, deputed his assistant to go up on the stage with his apologies. She should, he said, demand a little more restraint and patience. Busi would not let them down. But this was not an audience that was greatly charmed by her demands. In their own homes and offices, they *made* demands; they didn't do what they were told, they didn't show restraint. Why should they do so here, especially when clapping with two hundred others of their class was so much fun?

Now the throng of freeloaders in the gardens were pressing

even more at the marquee entrances, attracted by the wealthy noise as moths are drawn to Mona's lamp. Some of them stepped inside. When attendants asked them to move away, they held their ground. These were public gardens, after all. A bit of canvas couldn't take away their rights. There was some shoving and a punch. A couple from the Shabs with aching knees spotted a pair of empty seats, just vacated by the young men standing and displaying at the front, and so they hurried forward to relax in them. A man—a mendicant, in fact, who'd only just been turfed out of his shelter in the other Gardens for his night on the streets—saw and took an opportunity for lifting bags and pickpocketing. Another, sporting a woman's scarf in saffron silk as a rakish kerchief, patrolled the gangways in between the seats hoping to spot, for later, someone as battered and defenseless as the man he'd robbed that very afternoon, a man he'd never thought to see again. The frontiers of the marquee had been breached. The outside was sending in its tired, its poor, its huddled masses, the wretched refuse of our teeming shore.

A large part of the audience closest to the makeshift stage was now standing up and turning round to watch the fracas at the back. "They'd better fetch some constables," somebody said. And Joseph—beyond his mother's hearing, thankfully—repeated to his companions the phrase he'd used with Soubriquet earlier that week: "Unruly dogs. They should be whipped." The young men who had lost their seats elbowed back to reclaim them, fists already raised in case the old folk wouldn't yield. A couple of hotheads in the unfixed seating at the rear waved their chairs in the air, in solidarity.

*

We have to thank a young musician known then—and now—by the single name of *Cedric* for bringing this disorder to a halt. *Cedric* played piano accordion, and was being paid only an apprentice fee for helping out with the accompaniments on those few songs for which Busi preferred to abandon the grand piano and stand at the microphone, closer to his listeners. The accordion was the most heartfelt of the instruments in *Cedric*'s view and one that, unlike any other instrument he knew of—with the exception of the bagpipes, possibly, and some percussion sets—required its master or its mistress to move in three directions at once. It was, he said, like patting your head, rubbing your stomach, and shaking your dick at one go. Except with the accordion the challenge was to finger keys, to squeeze the lungs, and to select the chord buttons simultaneously, and not lose any tempo while you're doing it.

Now here was an unexpected chance for *Cedric* to make a name for himself. His instrument was strapped around his shoulders, a large and heavy encumbrance, so he was ready to perform. He was himself a little perplexed by the absence of the master singer and composer. Busi had a reputation for reliability, an early man who never hurried off, but had an encore for the crowd and autographs for everyone. The marquee manager had telephoned the singer's home but there had been no reply. Of course, the organizers understood the maestro was elderly. They needed no reminding—as most of them were readers of *Indices*—that Busi had endured an awful week. In fact, they half expected him to cancel earlier, especially once they'd seen the photograph and all those dreadful bandages and wounds. But there had been no word. Their confidence in him had grown.

Not to show up and not to give them any warning was unusual and alarming. Something must have happened to the man.

Something had to happen in the marquee too. *Cedric* had been waiting out of sight to the side of the stage when the mayhem started to break out. When the manager saw the young men racing to reclaim their seats from some rough shoddies from the town, and then saw grown men throwing punches in the front row, he gave *Cedric* quite a shove in the small of the back and said, "Play now, for goodness sake! Play loud."

Terina was more alarmed and more informed than any other member of the audience, of course. Busi's nonappearance was not a great surprise, she supposed. She'd seen the sorry state of him that afternoon in town. She'd studied what he'd studied in the arcade window and could easily imagine the anger he might feel if the building plans were not already known to him. It was little wonder that he'd taken to his bed to sulk. It must have been a ghastly week for him. He would not want to stand onstage and sing of love when all he felt was deepening dismay. She would not want to listen to him sing.

Terina had made her mind up, before the fracas in the marquee escalated into something more than noise, that as soon as she could get away she'd find a taxi and go down to the villa on the waterfront. Her intended quarrel with Joseph could sit and simmer until another time. Quite honestly, she was relieved at that. Alfred could be fast asleep by now, spark out and resting his old bones, but if there was a burning light in any of the rooms or any sound, she would step up to that grand front door and knock. If there were no answer, she knew where her sister had secreted a spare key. She'd shoot the lock and step inside that damp and gloomy little lobby with its clutter of old coats and parasols. Then she could imagine slipping off her nice new shoes to creep upstairs as noiselessly as some small girl playing hide-and-seek, or some late teenager, hoping not to wake a parent, but knowing that the parents would not sleep until their child was home. She imagined Busi's bandaged face pressed into the pillows. Would she crane to listen for his breathing? Perhaps he'd snore and set her mind at rest. But, if he didn't, would she cross the room in her bare feet to check that Alfred Busi was alive?

She could not help but think that Joseph really wouldn't care if his uncle breathed no more. He might be glad. After all, she and her son were Busi's only family and, if there was any order in the world, they would be his heirs. The villa would be theirs. That must have played a part in Joseph's plan—to have his uncle dead, and then possess his property; and benefit from royalties, of course. Would she care much herself, Terina wondered, if indeed she did find Alfred lifeless in his bed? Would she dare to touch his face or hand to see if he was warm or cold or somewhere in between? Would she then apply her lips to his and hope to breathe him back to life? Wasn't that what you were meant to do? Would she push up his clothes to lean with pressure on his chest until she had him gasping, turning blue to pink? She'd had him gasping once before, his clothes pushed up beneath her hands, she very well recalled; sex and death, equally breathless and grimacing, and equally demeaning. But, no, she truly wanted him alive, if only so he'd live to hear and believe that she had not betrayed him or her sister with these plans to build where he had always lived. She had to concentrate, despite the ugly racket in the marquee, despite the shouting and the claps, to rehearse what she might say to him that night, to make a list of what she should explain.

She had not made much progress when once again the man called Soubriquet approached. Out of nowhere, he was standing at her knees, so close to her that the frieze of stars around her hem was shaded by his trousers. He gave his business card to her and said, "I'd love an interview." Joseph hadn't noticed yet. He and his male friends, the twins included, were standing with their knees against their seats and with their backs to the stage, watching the fisticuffs and unruliness at the rear and sides of the marquee. This concert was turning out to be more diverting than they could have hoped. But it was only moments before he saw the journalist. His mother had hardly had the time to ask, "What interview?"

Everyone who witnessed this second act of the contretemps between the Press and Trade that Saturday—and that included many of the ticketless—would swear that both men raised their fists. Indeed, there was a photograph taken by a woman with one of those cheap Rolls Rollax cameras that later proved that fact. Joseph Pencillon, his face twisted upward and tilted toward the lens, was captured with his arm thrown back. He'd formed a fist, made all the more lethal by the rings he wore and by the heavy key chain he was holding in his palm. You could see the links glinting in the photographic print. Soubriquet was turned away, but swinging forward for the fight. You could not see his face—he'd later claim, in print, he hadn't even been at the concert—but you could see his fast-descending fist. It is disputed, though, whether or not either punch landed on its intended victim. Joseph—regretting that he hadn't been able to poke a shotgun

at the scoundrel's skull—would maintain he knocked out Soubriquet with one neat blow. If he did, there's no proof. Terina
couldn't see from where she sat. The journalist was in her way.
And, truly, hardly anybody else was watching anymore.

There'd been a startling blast of music, chilling in its sudden-
ness. The clamor in the marquee instantly reduced. A young man
no one recognized, though several of the younger people there
thought for a while that it was *Mister Al* himself, had stepped
up to the cliff edge of the stage, encumbered by an accordion
as shiny as a fairground carousel, and played the unmistakable
clarion of Busi's thrilling "Babel, Babel." At last, a concert had
begun. The young man was the herald of the star. Now everyone
expected *Mister Al* to step onstage dramatically, just when his
singing should begin. He'd waltz the stand just as he always did
and almost kiss the membrane of the microphone with all those
soft, seductive *b*'s: "Babel, Babel / hubbub of hell . . ."

But *Mister Al* did not step up to take command of anything.
Nobody came to sing that night. The only entertainment there
was *Cedric* No-name, squeezing out his repertoire of Busi songs,
and then, responding to applause, fetching from the side of the
stage his smaller cordionette to shrug off compositions of his
own. He did not sing but matched the music with expressions on
his face, a master class in rapture and elation. Besides, the melodies would not be made any richer by a lyric. They were already
as fully lunged and conversational as any voice. His instrument
was like a beating and inhaling chest, a rib cage making magic
on the stage. Who'd have thought a squeeze-box could produce
such sorcery? It helped that his good looks were of the flamboy-
ant kind and that he was young and tall. But, even if the audience
had been blind to his physical attractions, not one of them would

say the evening had been ruined or that the absence of the maestro had been a disappointment. No, they could say they'd been
there on the night when our town produced another, younger
maestro they could love. Nobody would have called for it to
end—Saturdays are made for encores; no one has to work next
day—and *Cedric*, *Cedric* the Peacemaker, *Cedric* the Wizard of
the Stomach, Head, and Dick, would go back that night to his
small room knowing that his talent had been recognized.

9

THEY SAT TOGETHER in the drawing room, the one below the balcony. It had not been much visited of late, even though in daytime it offered the best and brightest outlook from the ground floor, for anybody standing up, that is. Its chairs and sofas were old and saggy and so low that the windowsills obstructed the view of the promenade, the pebble beach, the sea. Busi had dragged his duet stool across from his practice room and set a little table at their feet with two of Alicia's green glass tumblers on it and the Boulevard bottle. He made sure, though, that the woman from next door did not take Alicia's place, on his left, but sat at his right shoulder. She was spread-eagled like a man, her knees set wide apart. Busi was crossed-legged at the ankle and hunched forward with his hands caught between his knees. It was just as well, he thought, that they were talking in a darkened room. In that brief corridor of light and time between letting in his visitor at the kitchen door, touring her around the house, and reaching the drawing room, he'd been reminded what a wreck he was. He was still muddied by the day, still shoeless, wounded, bruised, and swathed in bandages that should by now have been either replaced or washed.

She said her name was Alexandra, though only strangers called her that, and aunts and uncles. She much preferred to be known as Lexxx. She spelled it with a triple x because she liked the drama of having kisses in her name. Of course, she explained, you can't pronounce all three of the x's, "So who's to know?" But knowing they were there was satisfying, she explained, and made Busi try saying "Lexxx," pronouncing every x. She was correct, he admitted straightaway, baffled by the woman's scatter-gun conversation. Had she come this late to tell him this? An x was not a letter he could lengthen, shorten, or even double up. He could not think of any note on the piano he could not lengthen if he wanted to, though he could think of words in lyrics that it was never wise to stretch: *love*, for instance; *dead*. That was something that had not occurred to him before in almost fifty years of writing songs: music's water; words are stone.

Lexxx, of course, had spotted at once the state her neighbor was in but she would keep that to herself. She had not tried to tidy Busi up at the kitchen door or scurry round as Terina would have done, assembling her stinging salves or cutting strips of bandaging, then scolding him. She'd seen him stumbling down the promenade that late afternoon, caught up in the sudden storm, without his shoes and looking like he'd been on one almighty binge, reduced and lamed by alcohol or dope. This surely couldn't be the same man she'd met just a few days previously, the one with all the medals and the baggy suit but with the added oddity of wounds and dressings on his face. "That old fellow's *Mister Al*," one of her housemates had told her after that first meeting. "He's got a concert at the town hall on Saturday. You can stand outside for free." But the name did not resound with her. Her tastes were vocal jazz and opera, from a diva preferably, not from some buffo with a bloodied face.

But knowing that the injured and disheveled neighbor shambling through the rain had once been a famous singer of some sort, a troubadour, old-fashioned though that was, had left her curious and anxious. She could not imagine him recovering sufficiently to be onstage that evening, unless of course that was the way these performers prepared themselves and overcame their nerves—by getting spliced on stimulants and weather, by getting three sheets to the wind. Whatever she might make of him, in this new shabby guise, she certainly was curious to poke her nose into his life. Whereas he hadn't seemed worth knowing when he was stiffly dressed, flinching even when she'd held his arm in the street outside the Pastry House, he was now a mystery to be solved and a secret to be shared. She would step beyond her own musical arena for once and walk up to the concert venue. How would she pass the evening otherwise? She'd had a boring day, so nothing *Mister Al* might offer could worsen that. Her housemates were avoiding her again, and who could blame them? She was not mad exactly but, as she knew very well herself—she cultivated it, in fact—she certainly was unnerving company. She talked in salvos, laughed too much, made friends and enemies too readily, was loud.

It was not until the first blows in the marquee had been thrown, and some time before young *Cedric* commandeered the stage, that it dawned on Lexxx that her faltering neighbor would not be performing that evening. She'd been stupid to imagine that he could. Instead of coming up to hear him sing, she should have rescued him.

So young Lexxx, the Pastry House's most exasperating resident, for her housemates anyway, stepped down from the civic garden wall, from where she'd had a narrow, angled view into the concert tent, and shouldered her way through the crowd of ticketless concertgoers who were pressing forward in the hope of witnessing and maybe taking part in the fracas within. She knew a quick route down to the promenade that took her through the Shabs and the Shods—not quite the route that Busi had taken that afternoon, but similar. It would bring her to the oceanfront at the same place, by the old aquarium. The way would not be easy. It was night. There were no streetlamps. What light there was—in people's rooms—was low and flickering and did not squander any of its warmth or radiance outside.

Of course, she ought to keep well clear of neighborhoods like these. Their streets were dangerous. Not only might she fall and hurt herself, she also risked assault or robbery, especially on a partly moonlit night like this, when she'd be visible in silhouette from time to time. But Lexxx had never feared attack. She'd not been bullied once, at school, although she'd been the awkward sort of girl that normally would have attracted the mockers and the pinchers. She had a tongue on her and could protect herself with it. Any bruises she received would mend more quickly than the hurt she could inflict with words, when pressed. Anyway, why should she fear the townspeople who lived in these dark streets, any more than she should fear those rich young men she'd witnessed taking their seats in the marquee with their vast faces, overfed and pampered? She'd rather spend an evening with a family in the Sords than go near one of those violently lit bars where moneyed men stood at the doors to watch the women walking by. She'd had that pleasure far too many times and endured them passing judgment on her looks and figure. "No, thank you, Chubs," one man had called out, only a few evenings previously, as she came into view. "Find yourself a squirrel," she had said, to laughter from his compadres. No, she would rather avoid the wider streets and boulevards, where there were unruly men, especially on Saturdays.

Lexxx had been walking for only twenty minutes when she reached the entry to the Mendicant Gardens. There were vehicle lights outside and council motorvans. Within the gates she could see the lanterns of the constables, their long nightsticks and shorter truncheons already drawn. That evening's evictions were coming to a close. Quite soon the Gardens would be padlocked against everything but bats. She crossed onto the dark side of the street; it's never wise to show yourself to constables. Ahead of her, a family of mendicants, their bags and blankets in their arms, were heading for the promenade, where, tides permitting, they could scoop out pebble cots and beds below the storm defenses, out of the wind and out of sight, they hoped. In just a few hundred paces she would be home herself, and safe.

What was Lexxx hoping for or fearing when she stepped across the shared yard between the Pastry House and Busi's villa to knock on his kitchen door? That he'd not be dead, of course, although that was not a distant likelihood. It certainly would be his best excuse for not having come to sing. That possibly he'd taken to his bed and needed warming up and feeding? She could manage that. That he was crazy, some old sod who liked to be expected but took cheap pleasure in not showing up? She could identify with such behavior. Her own father had been the same. That he was gripped by sickness of some kind? She'd call a doctor or an ambulance. But most of all she hoped she'd find an old and interesting man who only wanted company. And that he'd share his drink with her. The walk had left her dry-mouthed and in need of alcohol.

*

Busi had not gone downstairs to let her in when she had pounded on his door that final time. He was not feeling well enough to negotiate the stairs again. He pushed the little bedroom window open to call out and ask what she wanted. She was sitting half perched on his refuse bin, waiting for an answer at the door and fussing one of the cats, a spiny gray. She looked up at the rattle of the window frame and blessed him with her wonky smile. He could not help but think of the last wild creature he had seen down there and sense that this young woman and the boy were somehow linked.

"What is it, then?" he called to her.

"I want to see inside," she said. She had to improvise a reason for her visit. Perhaps there'd been no cause to worry after all. "Is yours like mine? Your home, I mean. Not your insides." She grimaced at the very thought of it.

Busi was surprised, of course, and suspicious. Why would she want to see inside his home? It was not beyond the realms of cunning that Joseph Pencillon had sent her round to . . . what? To suggest that somebody as old and frail as he must appear to be that evening would benefit from living in a smaller place? Anyone might be in his nephew's pay. And so he hardly spoke to her as they went from room to room. She was showing exaggerated interest, he judged. It was as if, in preparation for what she had to do to earn her pay, she was inspecting the villa, noting its too high ceilings and its heavy doors, its ancient and complaining floorboards and its sagging plaster walls, its vague and salty dampness, the general sense of disrepair and underuse, the smell, the effort of the stairs, the half-forgotten rooms, the vast expense of making it contemporary.

"I'm planning to move out myself," he said, testing her reactions, when finally they reached the corridor between what had once been his boyhood music room and his parents' dressing room. "At least, I'm thinking of it."

"What, selling up?"

"Yes, like the Pastry House." He echoed what she'd said to him out on the promenade. "It's coming down. The lot. It's as good as pastry crumbs."

"But you were born here, weren't you?"

"Yes, I was—in that bedroom off this very corridor. In that same bed."

"Then, I'd have thought you'd want to stay . . . to end your days . . ." She'd gone too far, perhaps.

". . . in that same bed?"

"Our best lives are circles, are they not?" She'd read as much, just that morning, in Mondazy's *Truisms*. Now our town's philosopher could redeem her indiscretion.

Busi nodded, because, although he did not know precisely what she meant, he was now sure she was not in Joseph's pay.

"Let's drink to that," he said, suddenly glad to have her company. "Let's drink to my dry corpse on that old bed."

"May that circle not be closed too soon," she said, and laughed with pleasure at the neatness of her phrase.

*

Now in the darkness of the drawing room, on his long stool, the bottle was almost drained. Lexxx had never tasted Boulevard Liqueur before and wouldn't seek it out again. "It's 'Spirited from Nature,'" she said, reading from the label. But it was potent, no matter what it tasted of. She could not decide whether it was figs or some sugary reduction of rubber.

"It's mulberry," her neighbor said.

"It doesn't look like mulberry," she replied, holding it up to the moonlight. "It isn't red. It's green."

"That's the glass that's green."

"Well, then, it doesn't smell like mulberry." She made a show of sniffing it, then emptying the glass.

"The label says it's mulberry."

"The label must know best, of course." She had to laugh. She'd had such aimless conversations many times before, but thanks to hashish, not to mulberry.

"I see you've finished it, rubbery or not."

"I'm fond of rubbery."

Now her neighbor was laughing too, though wincing at the mouth while doing so. Their prattle was ridiculous; this was the way young people spoke but rarely men of his age. "In that you're not unlike my wife, Alicia," he replied. "She loved her Boulevard Liqueur. She's been gone for almost two years now. I mean she died; she didn't run away. And we have finished off the final bottle that she left behind. Adieu."

So Lexxx inquired about Alicia, as she must, and had the grace to stay attentive even when Busi, his tongue loosened by the darkness and the alcohol, and by the unusual warmth of the ample body to his right, began to repeat his memories and then allowed himself to weep, too silently to hear, but she could feel the shudders in his shoulder and his knees. Afterward, to bring him back, she wondered how his career in singing had been carved out, against the odds. ("Ah, yes. My father always said, 'Songs will never stock a pantry.'") And then they sympathized about the villas: Lexxx hadn't heard about the larger scheme, The Grove, that would be built. And then at last she felt that they were close enough for her to ask exactly how he'd ended up so wounded and so derelict. So dirty too. And he told her everything: the bins, the boy, the bite, the beating, and the Pencillons. He pointed to the spot where he'd been punctured and the place where he'd been punched. He finished up by recounting his last dream to her, making it more orderly and meaningful. "Our streets were teeming with the animals," he said. "You couldn't take a step for fear of treading on a tail." She nodded, laughed, and smiled at everything he said. She'd heard the nighttime racket at the bins a hundred times. She'd spotted animals. The contents of his dreams were not so very strange to her. He'd never been so listened to since Alicia had died, not even on the stage. This young woman—and their tumblers full of rubber— had restored his buoyancy.

"I was at the concert, earlier," she said. "I didn't stay. I guessed you wouldn't sing."

Busi hardly dared to ask what had happened in his absence. Was it chaos? Was he missed? Was there a decent audience, or empty seats? Were people saying he had let them down, disgraced himself? He didn't get the chance to speak, because Lexxx had taken hold of his elbow and was pointing out into the street. "There's someone there," she said. "Who's she?"

"Stay still," he told her. "We can't be seen. She isn't welcome here."

Terina had come down by cab as soon as *Cedric* had completed the first half of his concert. She would've stayed if only, for the second time that day, she hadn't felt the tug of duty demanding that she chase after Alfred yet again. She took some pleasure in the anxiety she hoped her hasty, unexplained departure would cause for Joseph. He might have thought she'd gone off to the ladies' or for an interval stroll in the gardens, but would now, with any luck, be sitting next to her empty chair in the second half of the concert, not knowing what had happened to his mother. He was too conventional to leave the marquee while the youth was playing his accordion. He'd already made a blustering fool of himself that evening with the journalist and would not want to be noticed a third time, making a display, offending protocols. He'd choose to keep his seat, she was certain of that. Well, let him stew. Let him work out for himself how he'd offended her.

She was worried and surprised to find that the Busi house was dark. During the drive through the thronging boulevards and along the promenade, she had not dared to think the worst: that her brother-in-law had had a seizure of some kind, a stroke, a fit, a heart attack, or—more likely, given his most recent moods—a breakdown or eruption. Something truly drastic must have prevented him from turning up at the marquee for what would have been one of the most important concerts of his career. It had been organized just to honor *Mister Al* in the week of his accession to the Avenue of Fame. Now the lack of light in any of the villa's rooms was alarming. Where was he, if he wasn't in the house? He hadn't any friends to hide away with, as far as she could tell, especially on this Saturday evening. All his colleagues and acquaintances—the other musicians of the town, the owners of the café where he sang these days, those twins who lived next door when they were children, even the writer from *Indices*—had been invited to the concert and all had turned up, seemingly. There was not a single empty seat—and there were crowds outside, hoping to listen for free.

Well, then, Alfred, surely, had to be inside the house and either dead in darkened rooms or too unwell to work the switch. This—whatever it would prove to be—was Joseph's fault. And, she feared, her own. So she was ready for the worst but in no hurry to encounter it. The last dead body she'd seen, many years ago, had been her husband's, but only after he had been discovered, then prepared and dressed by their two maids. She'd never had to deal with slumps before. What if she had to give the kiss of life? The thought was not appealing.

She crossed the road and stood with her back to the pebble beach and the ocean to see more clearly into the villa's rooms. There was sufficient moonlight to alleviate their darkness. She could make out the glint of mirrors, the ghostly shroud of curtains, the outline of some of Alicia's vases on the windowsills. She listened too, half hoping that Alfred was in that back room where he played piano, with the door shut tight, all light contained within. All she heard was traffic, weather, and the sea. It was only when she crossed the promenade again that she thought she caught a movement in the window of the ground-floor drawing room below the balcony. She stopped dead in her tracks. Any vehicle would have knocked her to the ground. But there was nothing to be seen. No sign of life. All she could make out was what looked like either the high back of a couch or two bodies sitting closely, side by side, as still as furniture.

The Busis had an ostentatious brass bell with a Latin tag around its rim: QUI ME TANGIT VOCEM MEAM AUDI, "Whoever strikes me, hears my voice." Alicia had brought it back from their honeymoon in Venice. The salesman said it was an antique *campanello* and from the gateway to a demolished monastery along the coast in Trieste. But there were several other identical bells throughout the town, bought not in Venice but in Algiers or Beirut or Amsterdam. It swung from a weighted pendulum so that in the worst of storms it rang itself like a ship's bell. "That's No One, seeking refuge from the wind," Alicia would say, but she would still not settle until she'd gone to open up the door and announce, "No One's gone away again."

Terina pulled the bell's brass chain a bit too heavily and surprised herself with its stridency. The sound rang out across the street. It wasn't meant for discreet visitors, hoping not to be spotted by the locals. It was just as well the only neighbors were those young people in the Pastry House. "Deaf and noisy," Alfred said. When no one came, she tried a second time and waited for the sound to die and for the light to be switched on inside the hallway and the lobby. She was not a superstitious woman but she held her thumbs in the palms of her hands and counted up to a hundred and back, starting with her own age, before reluctantly running her fingers behind the doorframe to locate the hidden spare key. Her hands were shaking when she put it to the lock. Why should she not be fearful? Nothing told her all was well.

She did not close the door behind her. Rather, she wedged it open with a copper umbrella bucket so that, if she needed it, her escape route back into the safety of the night was unimpeded.

She had not admitted it even to herself, but the attack on Busi at the larder door a few nights previously had unnerved her. She'd done her best to persuade herself and her brother-in-law that the wounds were consistent with nothing more unexpected than a cat, though privately she had thought otherwise. As Alfred had pointed out himself, the bite marks were flat and curved like a human mouth and jaw. So it was possible the human had returned to finish off his attack and might be waiting in the house for her. She had forewarned him with the bell and would continue to do so with the clipping of her tight new shoes on Alfred's wooden floors. She slipped them off and pushed them with her stockinged toes to the side of the open door and took hold of the heaviest of the umbrellas in the stand. She held it at the pointed, furled end, ready to defend herself with the hefty handle. She proceeded as silently as was possible with breathing as loud and panicky as hers and ran her spare hand along the wall of the hallway until she located the first light switch. The villa suddenly was large and twice as frightening. She listened carefully and heard what Alfred and Alicia had always heard: the haphazard music of a living house, the wheezing and the fidgeting, the muttering, the thuds. Everything seemed full of breath and blood.

Terina tiptoed first into the kitchen. The larder door was closed, but the bolt on the outer door that led to the little communal yard and the waste bins had been drawn back. Alfred might be outside, she thought. She could picture him—in his pajamas, for some reason—concussed and bleeding, just alive, spread out on the flagstones. He'd have something at his throat, an animal. She opened the door just a little, but there was no one there. A cat ran up and tried to arch its way inside; Terina stooped to block its head and keep it out, then shut the bolt, washed off the hint of mucus from the cat from her hands, and went to turn on the lights in the nearest downstairs rooms. The house, so far as she could tell, was empty, uninhabited—though from the outside it might now seem to anybody passing by that the Busi villa was hosting some great party of Invisibles. Most of the downstairs rooms were lit, and soon the upstairs rooms were glowing too. There was no sign of Alfred in his bed. The sheets were tidily and tightly drawn. The other rooms were empty and seemingly untouched. She saw the dust across their floors. No one had swept them, even with their socks, for many weeks. She left the lights to burn and occupy the house. A warm and yellow rhombus of illumination spread halfway across the street.

Terina was still perplexed but more relaxed. The villa, so far, seemed secure; she had only to check the two rooms at the end of the downstairs corridor, the practice room, where Alfred kept his music and his instruments—and Alicia's ashes—and that uncomfortable drawing room at the front, where no one ever sat but where she had imagined seeing movements earlier. That's when she heard the whispering.

At first, Terina thought the whispering had to be from off the street, because it was a woman's voice. Alfred had no women in his life, except her. Then she saw the pair standing darkly at the far end of the corridor between the practice room and the drawing room looking straight at her and seeming, even though their faces were unlit, sheepish and embarrassed. She could not help herself: she let a little scream escape and dropped the umbrella noisily. It clattered onto the floor and so surprised her that she let go a second, lesser scream. Those two figures were a jolt. They seemed so ghostlike and unreal. She had to press both hands against her chest to keep the shock contained and hold herself steady. Had she imagined them? Had she imagined that her sister had come back to life and was standing with her husband in her house? She looked again, as full of hope as fear. No, it was not Alicia. The figure was too square-set and too young. But it was Alfred, certainly.

"What is it that you want?" he asked, with more aggression than she'd ever known from him. That was his voice for sure. Though who she was, the huddled mass beside him that she had mistaken for a ghost, Terina couldn't even guess. Clearly she had caught them out. So Alfred had a piece of skirt, was that the phrase? It was not possible that this woman was a proper lover of some kind, a future wife, whom her brother-in-law had kept secret rather than reveal he had finally *betrayed* Alicia. This body was too young. What, then? A prostitute? Some reckless fan? Some casual pick-up from a bar who in repayment for a drink and food might do what Terina had done herself so many years before, and play around with *Mister Al*?

The mystery would only deepen when she reached out for the wall switch and lit up the far end of the corridor. She was not prepared for what she saw. Alfred was even more disheveled than he'd been that afternoon outside Joseph's offices, much grubbier. He had a further injury to his forehead, a lid of raw flesh, a heavy gash of blood. The dressings she had prepared for him and applied so carefully were grimy and dislodged. His clothes were filthy, caked in mud. His feet were bare and soiled. His body was misshapen too. It sagged. It was as if he had no working bones. The woman at his side was clean but just as ungainly in her way, Terina thought. At least she'd not been caught undressed. Imagine that! She wore a pair of Tyrol boots and one of those shapeless studio smocks with a shoulder halter much favored by the students at the Conservatoire and by larger girls. Hers was the color of unfired clay and could suit nobody. Her hair, if it was loose or tied, might be pretty, given half a chance. But when it was piled like this, she looked as if she had a bread roll on her head. Her statement to the world was brown. She'd be about a third of Alfred's age. And, more than that, the pair of them looked drunk. And sounded it.

"What is it that you want?" he said again. "Who let you in?"

"I used my sister's key, the hidden one," she said, not meaning to lay claim to the villa but simply to explain herself. "And who is this? I'm sorry to disturb you both, of course." She would have turned and left the villa before the answer came. She recognized the anger in the house, and even guessed its provenance. Explanations—and apologies—from both sides would come later, she was sure. All she wanted now was to reclaim her pretty shoes and escape. Caruso was waiting on the gramophone. She'd find some solace in his voice after an evening in which no solace was available. She'd already let out two screams that evening, and now she shed her first small tear. Alfred's rudeness was distressing, and unfair.

Before she had the chance to turn away, the clay-and-bread-roll girl had sped along the corridor in her unwieldy boots and had her arms around Terina's shoulders. Lexxx'd always been the one when she was young to give comfort to her younger sisters and her weeping mother. She understood—she had been told on the piano stool—why her neighbor was so distrustful of his sister-in-law, but tears come first. Sorrow outplays anger every time.

10

THERE WAS HARDLY ROOM on Busi's duet stool for three, but that is where they ended up, with Lexxx sitting grandly, her knees spread wide as if she were the only person in the world, between the bony bottoms of her neighbor and his sister-in-law. There had not been an argument. No one truly wanted one. That womanly embrace in the corridor had delivered Busi back to his kinder self, no longer selfishly involved but sympathetic now for someone else. She looked so lost and oh so very short without her shoes, just like a waif. He'd had to close the gap and put his arm around Terina's shoulder in the spaces left by Lexxx. If Alicia had been alive, she would have poked her husband from behind and told him, "Go." In fact, she'd said the week she died, "Be sure Terina is okay. Take care of her." That had been her one request, so Alfred really had to honor it by joining in the hug.

Their awkward six-limbed huddle formed a pocket of warm air and a tangle of affection, blind to the world. The three of them had closed their eyes, so forgiveness had been brokered only by touch. Busi blushed just to think how he'd spoken to Terina, how unforgiving he had been, when he'd seen her standing in his home a few moments earlier, that umbrella in her hand and pinched with fear, just as he'd been himself the day he blooded Simon Klein. "Who let you in?" he'd shouted cruelly—when it had been only a few days since he had phoned her in the darkest hours of the night, when she was sleeping, to beg for help. He was glad that nobody could see the shame on his face. He had it pressed into the embroidered shoulder of Terina's street coat. He'd made himself invisible.

She had explained, of course: a blurting list of what she hadn't done and what she didn't know. There'd been no family plot, no secrecy. The world—the business world, that is—was simply spinning round and trading what-has-been for what-must-be. She didn't understand its values but she recognized its strength. There can't be any progress without change. But it was hard for her to implicate her son, particularly as in her heart she was ashamed of him—and shame is something that a mother doesn't want to share. So Busi did his best to seem entirely unperturbed by what he had discovered in the office window that morning. He'd known all about it, actually, he said. The company had written to him many times with details of The Grove. She could see the opened letters herself if she wanted. He'd been offered "a very stately set of rooms, with ocean views, just like the views I have already." They'd offered two apartments, actually, one to own and one to rent. There had even been a thoughtful, hand-written note from Joseph himself: "Uncle, this is wonderful."

Indeed, it sounded wonderful, in Busi's tailored version. He could almost fool himself into believing all his dealings with The Grove and with its several partners had been open and direct. What was certain was that, now that he'd lied so generously

about the development of the bosk for Terina's sake, he had also
slammed a door on himself and could not open it again. He could
hardly say, on some other less stressful occasion, "Oh, by the
way, those shysters had me for a fool. I lied to you, because I
was ashamed, because I doubted you and raised my voice."
Nor could he express either to his nephew or to his sister-in-law
the anger he had felt, the hatred. No, he had charmed himself
into the basket woven for the snake and pulled the lid across.
His feeble decency had ensnared him. What had Terina said?
Something like: We all want progress but we can't stand change.
We want to keep what we have had and loved; we want to grasp
what's new and lovable. That, exactly as she'd said, was how the
great world spins.

"I cannot offer alcohol," he'd said at last to Terina, pulling
back from the two women in the corridor and blinking at the
light. "We finished it." In fact, he couldn't offer anything. His
widower's larder was almost empty.

"Well, that's a pity. It has been a very thirsty Saturday so
far." She stood back herself and brushed out the creases in her
dress, which she imagined must have come while they embraced.
"You might have tea?"

"I have a bottle of wine," Lexxx said. "Or at least one of my
housemates does. It could be something cheap and rough. I'll
fetch it, shall I? Let's hope he isn't there to see me steal it." She
released one of her thunderbolting laughs. "Whoops-me."

Busi went down the hallway into the lobby to close the front
door and switch off some of the lights his uninvited visitor had left
blazing. He'd like to return the house to darkness once again and
sit once more—with friends and family—on that long stool to

watch the ocean through the villa's windowpanes. He came back with Terina's shoes, held by their dainty heels. He didn't like to see her in bare feet. That imperfection did not flatter her, not in the way that imperfections flattered Lexxx. That young woman might not be elegant or shapely, she might not be an arbiter of fashion, but she had made the opposite—the homespun look, her brusquerie of dress—a challenge and a pleasure to behold. You could not put a woman such as that in heels. And thinking that reminded Busi of his own bare feet, of how he must appear to his meticulous sister-in-law, a ragamuffin dipped in mud.

He was about to say to her, "I need to change and wash," when he heard the kitchen door pulled open and looked up along the corridor to see his neighbor stepping out into the yard in search of wine. There was at once from her a cry of disbelief, of vindication possibly, and both Busi and Terina had time enough to look beyond Lexxx's shoulder into the almost blackness of the yard. And what they both saw, all too briefly, could never be a cat or a dog or even some great bird, descended from the firmament of giants. Nor could it be another visitor in clothes. In that split second they were sure that what they'd seen was naked flesh. How could anyone confuse a streak of naked flesh with cloth or fur or feathers?

They reached the open kitchen door in a heartbeat and stood at Lexxx's shoulder, looking out into the yard and then toward the escarpment, where they could hear the snap of tiny branches and the rustle in the undergrowth of naked, running feet. A few pieces of dry scree tumbled down the slope, then there was unbroken silence for a while, until an owl far off behind the villa inquired, "Who? Who?"

"He's gone," Lexxx said.

"You think it was the boy?" Terina could no longer talk of cats. She had seen for herself what Alfred had now encountered twice.

"It absolutely was a boy. I had a perfect view of him."

"And he was naked?"

"Bare as a bald man's head." She stepped farther into the yard. The bins were upended and rolling on their sides. Something had dragged out the contents and spread them on the flagstones and in the drainage gutters. The ground was tainted by the droppings and the pellets of a dozen animals, from mice to cats to deer. Lexxx had to tiptoe through the mess in her ungainly boots. "There's been a feast tonight," she said. She looked up into the trees and shook her head, but she was evidently not shocked by what or who she'd seen. When she spoke later to her friends, she'd say, "We were moving on from Boulevard Liqueur to alcoholic vinegar. And it was night. So who's to know whose arse I saw?" But actually she knew it hadn't been a dream or a hallucination, because—she'd keep this secret, even from her old neighbor—the boy, the beast, had touched her as it sped away, transferring fear and hope onto her hand. His fingertip had brushed her knuckles, gently so, as if imploring her to keep his being to herself.

They passed that evening side by side, on Busi's stool, discussing anything except the fleeting glance they'd shared but were not certain they had shared. They talked about the changes there would be, how everything was coming down, how what you knew when you were young would disappear when you were gray, how sad it was to lose the trees, how wild the oceans would remain, no matter what, how old age was blizzarded with

all the debris of our days. They finished off the red wine Lexxx
had stolen from the Pastry House, although behind the green
glass of Alicia's tumblers it looked—and tasted—as brown as
peat. Terina described the mayhem in the marquee earlier that
evening and how the concert had been rescued by the young
man with the huge accordion. When Busi asked if he'd been a
worthy replacement for *Mister Al*, she'd had to say he wasn't any
good, "Not musical; he couldn't even sing."

Then, finally, when there was nothing else to drink and nothing else to say, except what they wanted to avoid, Terina called
a taxi and went home, accepting, as she stepped out through the
villa's antique door, a brotherly kiss on both cheeks from Busi
and another all-embracing hug from Lexxx. Then Lexxx herself
returned across the yard to her unmade bed in her damp room,
and left Busi once again alone. Busi's impulse was to bolt the
door against the creatures in the yard, against the violence in our
town, against the wind and any rain, but a greater urge, fortified
by all the alcohol he'd drunk, persuaded him to leave the back
door gaping wide. There was nothing he should fear, or nothing
worse anyway than what had already happened in the week. He
opened up the larder too, and as he walked away, grimly happy
with himself, he swung the chain of Persian bells, still hanging
from the hinges and the latch, and listened to the melody that no
one wrote, the song that had no words, the water that was waiting for its stone.

*

We leave him sitting in his drawing room, the midnight
widower. He has the wide stool to himself. He sits there look-

ing at the sea and stars until his head drops with exhaustion and his chin is rested on his chest. He's in between the dusk and the dawn, between the future and the past. He can either fall asleep and dream or he can stay awake and dream, all day, all night. That's what we're free to do. We are. We are. We are the animals that dream.

PART TWO

POVERTY PARK

———//———

11

MY NEIGHBOR and my landlord would prefer it if I called him "Alfred," even "Al," but the names stick in my mouth. He is even older—seventy today—than my own father; there's a man who cherishes formality and would not want his son to flout the protocols, again. I am, my papa says, "Too ready to be warm." Warmth is for women, in his view. I do my best, therefore, to placate him, even in his absence, by staying just a pace away from elders, my head respectfully inclined a degree or so, hoping to seem measured but not without charm. So I think my neighbor is resigned to being Mr. Busi when I call to sit beside him at his apartment's picture window and watch the ocean rolling in and out, protected from the weather by the modern, strengthened, deadened glass. We neither of us let our shoulders rub.

Lex, however—she's dropped the kisses from her name; her life is free of kisses, so she says—is not embarrassed by the familiarities. She's chummy and she's bold. He's always "Al" with her. So on those not so rare occasions when we two are together in Mr. Busi's company, there is an awkward discord when we speak; it is as if I am the young employee, fearful and respectful, and she the trusted confidante. But actually the opposite is true. I am the confidant when she's not around; it is with me that Mr. Busi shares the story of his life, the story that I have recounted here. Once in a while, when he senses all his neighbors have gone out, I can persuade him to lift the fallboard of his vintage upright and perform his songs, the music anyway; he will not sing. And he will show his photographs and composition sheets to me. I invite him to reveal himself. Despite my distance and formality, I can ask him anything—*because* of them perhaps—and he answers. "We must swap stories," he said when we first met, an inviting phrase, but what he really meant was: "Let me tell you mine."

With Lex, he is the listener. She loves to talk and share her day. I've heard her call him "Papa" once or twice and noticed that he always swells and preens on hearing it. I half suspect he sees us as his children, his adopted son and daughter, though how that meshes with another stronger suspicion that he would like the two of us to be a pair I cannot bear to think about. He clearly has not wondered why it is that both of us, now no longer young, have not found spouses yet and, in public anyway, have no lovers. I cannot conceive of any quadranting of choices and desires that could place me in her arms or her in mine. I like her, though. I find it easy to be brotherly. We do not embrace, of course, and I can brush only her cheek with what is called a corpse's kiss, the opposite of smoldering. I must not seem "too ready to be warm" with anybody, young or old. However, I am not tempted to explain this fear of contact, especially to someone of Mr. Busi's age and so uxorious. He must have noticed, though, that the family table he has spread for Lex and me is not one at which I can be comfortable to dine.

A third suspicion is that my neighbor intends to leave us

money or some value in his will. More than once I've heard
him telling Lex his royalties will keep her fed. And "This will
be yours," he said to me on one occasion when I admired the
lithograph of St. Mark's he keeps in his kitchenette. I sometimes
wonder if that's his way of buying company and also if it's my
excuse for providing it so readily, so patiently. I can't pretend
the prospect of being Mr. Busi's beneficiary is not tempting. I'd
sit in his room and listen to his talk all day long if I was certain
of rewards—though I'm hoping, banking on, something more
than just one smudgy lithograph. However, I would be mortified
if anybody thought that profit and inheritance were the only reasons, since I became the tenant of his spare apartment about ten
months ago, that I have so regularly stepped across the corridor
to help him reminisce. My rooms are dark and claustrophobic.
My narrow open deck faces into the sheered wall of the escarpment, where the great claws of the site machines of The Grove
development ripped the landscape smooth and bare. Ferns and
mosses have already settled in the cracks and excavated spaces.
Occasionally, a scrub lizard lifts and jerks its head at me, and
there are roosting doves at night, but otherwise it feels as if I'm
living in a prison yard, with only a twenty-minute window of
bright light just after dawn. At other times, I have to switch on
lamps if I want to read or even check the color of my clothes. I
could be splashing in the shallows on the newly sanded beach
in just a minute or so, but, from my rooms, the ocean is remote.

Only once have I made the mistake of hanging my washing
out on the deck for it to dry. The clothes came back even damper
and limed by birds. I am always pleased on weekend mornings or
in the evenings when I return from the Academy and my stifling

pedagogic duties to call on Mr. Busi and borrow for an hour, say, his light, his chair, his view, his memories. He lets me festoon his little screened balcony with my washing. It has the sun and wind.

Today is Saturday and Mr. Busi's anniversary. His "gateway" anniversary. He has exhausted his three score years and ten and now must step—these words are his, an early song— "Into the meadows beyond the city walls / Where rivers hasten to their waterfalls / and drop." It has fallen to me to organize— at his sister-in-law's request—some celebrations, though doing that is not without its pitfalls. I have to be a diplomat. Mrs. Pencillon herself is hardly well enough to enjoy anything other than the lightest lunch, away from sunshine or from any drafts. Her son must be involved, of course, but only briefly. His uncle will be dutiful but cannot be expected to enjoy himself or even be himself while Joseph plays the host and condescends to all of us, though why he should I do not know—perhaps because he *almost* was elected as our mayor a year or so ago. I catch him staring at me when we meet as if he counts me as a puzzle or a threat. Perhaps, he half remembers seeing me, the night he used his gun.

Then there is Lex. She is not easy to accommodate. Terina— I would not address her as that to her face—is unexpectedly fond of the woman and seems to be enlivened by her scatty conversations and endlessly interested in the gypsy clothes she wears, but at any wider family gatherings Lex and the merchant-trader are bound to end up arguing. They are equally belligerent and stubborn. Mr. Busi describes them as "two clashing continents"— Antarctica and Africa, I think—and were never meant to share their borders or their temperatures.

My first suggestion was to take them all to somewhere where

the talking and the clashing would be limited. A summer concert seemed a good idea. *Cedric*, our great accordionist, "the Peacemaker," as he is promoted, is performing today, live on the bandstand in the botanic pastures as part of our solstice festival. We could all have had lunch in the garden restaurant there with our chairs angled toward the music and away from the tabletops over which arguments and differences, given half a chance and a couple of minutes of silence, were likely to squad up like armies in a battle. But I could tell that Mr. Busi did not want to be the devotee of someone else's talent, especially that young man's. "Ah, my usurper," he said when I proposed it, and shook his head. I don't think he likes to be seen about the town anyway, in case he's recognized, in case he isn't recognized.

Instead I have proposed, it being June and predictably dry and warm, to hire someone to drive us out of town to anywhere that Mr. Busi names for a picnic and some country air. He has, of course—I know his story now—said he'd like to visit, maybe for a final time, the clearings in Poverty Park, where—I'll not forget this blushing anecdote—he shamed himself with Simon Klein and where his wife preferred to picnic. "We went there just before she died," he tells me. Mr. Busi has the softest face— spongy, I would say—when he remembers these closing days with Alicia. "She was too ill to leave the back seat of the car, but we put all the windows down, wrapped her up in blankets, and let her feel the wind." By the time they had to go back home, her lap was full of leaves, he says. She told her husband that they really must come out again to the park on a less blustery day. He had taken that to be a sweetly optimistic plan, as if the future could promise her any *again*s. But afterward he realized she meant her ashes, not herself. That's why she didn't want a day with wind.

So that is what I have arranged, at his suggestion: a picnic and a scattering of ashes. But Mr. Busi would appreciate the outing all the more if only Lex and I were guests. This seems to me both flattering and chilly. It is a pity that the mother must be distanced like the son. Nevertheless, it is agreed, we will visit the Pencillons this morning on the way but keep the excursion and its second, greater purpose to ourselves. We cannot expect Terina, with her frail legs, to battle with uneven ground or tolerate the flies, and Joseph Pencillon does not possess a pair of shoes suitable for anything other than stepping from an office into a taxi, or from his Panache into a bank. He has insisted, though, on "obtaining"—not purchasing—the hamper. It can be his uncle's birthday gift. He will "supply," as well, his driver and his car.

Terina is not in bed when we arrive, but is dressed and sitting in a wicker chair shaded by phloteria and a blind vine on the patio of Joseph's residence, where she has a ground-floor room. *A suite*, according to her son. You would not know that she is ill or unable to stand without the help of somebody at her side, except that beneath the woolen throw over her legs her hands are constantly working on her knees, massaging the inflammation. In some respects, she grows more handsome by the week. The unforgiving pain whose company she keeps, all night, all day, has sculpted her. She has a dignity and eminence that wasn't there when we first met. I can imagine her in marble or in bronze, a Caesar's wife, the Empress Katerine. At first, I thought she was a mannequin, little more, one of those women who have sacrificed their lives to slenderness. She still dresses splendidly. She could illustrate an essay on Society or even represent the Elegance of Age in *Modenschau* magazine or *C'est la Mode*.

Today she wears a fox-fur stole that neatly hides her shoulder sag, over a cinnamon top. She has judged her makeup and her jewelry well. Flawless and restrained. She kisses both Lex and her brother-in-law, wrapping her lean arms around both of their shoulders in a hug as they stoop to greet her—but she offers me only her hand, which I am meant to take and hold, not kiss. She understands me all too well. Her kindness blesses me. A stranger, meeting her for the first time and mistaking clothes for skin, could not guess how fat and rich she is with tenderness, despite her chilly, mannered elegance. I have been Mr. Busi's companion on his twice weekly visits to her bedside over the last few months, and I've grown to love her, can I say? Not like a mother or an aunt. And not as a *marraine de la famille*. Or even as some sweetheart from a past I never have enjoyed. But something else, untempting and unvisited. A muse. Is that the word? A maharani and a muse, though what she will inspire in me or what I will create from her, I cannot tell just yet.

Lex wants to believe it was her own suggestion that we carry the coffer with Alicia's ashes out to the clearings at Poverty Park. I will not rob her of that illusion. Mr. Busi has been a widower for about eight years, she reminds him, bullies him, and he has often said that his wife requested to be scattered not on the beach by the promenade—she'd hate the newly imported sand—or in the sea, but under the trees, away from town, another fallen leaf among the millions. "Now's the day for it, Al," Lex said emphatically this morning. "Let's go, the three of us, and see her off, just as she wanted it." Surely he wouldn't let Alicia's mortal remains sit forever on his piano top "like a misplaced tea caddy," especially since the villa she once loved and shared has been destroyed and then replaced.

Lex is not the pious sort, but she enjoys a ceremony, she likes to stage a drama. Mr. Busi's birthday outing has been amplified, by her alone, she thinks, into a requiem with ashes: two lives are being celebrated instead of simply one. We can rely on Lex to turn the passions up. She has prepared a prayer, she says. She has bought some flowers too.

"We really have to make a . . ." I think she meant to say "a show of it," but stopped herself. "You'll want to make it memorable."

"Lest we forget," Mr. Busi said.

But Lex is deaf to irony. "We'll make it unforgettable," she promised him. "We'll take some offerings out to the forest. Something to keep her company, you know, like in the pyramids . . ." She did not seem to mind that we laughed.

"*Ushabtis* for the afterlife, you mean?" I said. "Something for the mummies?"

"Why not? We can bury what we take, under where you spread her ashes, Al."

"What offerings are those?" Mr. Busi put his hand onto her shoulder, to settle rather than restrain her.

"I'll help you choose. Just bury what belongs," she said, responding to his gesture by reaching out and cupping his elbow in her palm.

I stood aside. I played no part in that. Warmth is for women, I've been told. Nor did I help them pick through the drawers and boxes in his crowded rooms in search of offerings. I only watched. What is that English phrase? A second cook will not improve the soup? We have our own: "Too many fingers stop the dough from proving." I could have shouted out suggestions, but I preferred to witness—and predict—what Mr. Busi selected without my help. His first choice—and what could be more fitting?—was that spare villa key. "Might as well; it's got her fingerprints," he said. "Anyway, there's not a lock for it anymore. There's not a door. There's not even a home to open up." He has refused to think of his new apartment as a home, even though it and my rental across the corridor occupy almost exactly the same space as the middle upper-floor rooms of the old villa and enjoy the same views over the same ocean. "I'm homesick for the place I knew," he has said, even though he's living in it now.

Lex placed the key at the bottom of a wooden produce box she'd rescued from below his sink and lined—so fittingly again—with sheet music. Next, he chose the heavy brass bell with its Latin tag, the *campanello* that had once sounded in the wind outside the street door to their villa. "Whoever strikes me, hears my voice," Mr. Busi recited, as he explained that his wife had bought it on their honeymoon "for far more lire than it was worth. You'd think it was gold, not brass." He clacked it with the side of his wedding ring but could not summon a true note. "We'll take her Persian bells," he said, his final choice. "They ought to be with her. Besides, I haven't got a larder now—just that idiotic ice chest in my *galley*." He put the string of tiny bells into the offerings box, draped around the key and the *campenello*. They twinkled with both sound and light. He was not keen on Lex's suggestion, however, that he first break symbolically and then add the pieces of one of the antique crystal glasses Alicia had prized but hardly dared to use ("She wouldn't want me breaking up the set of six") or that he include a scarf she wore and that her husband had hung over his bedroom mirror ("Terina ought to have that, don't you think?") or the book of copied recipes in his wife's own hand that he kept in the kitchen ("I'll need that, if I ever mean to cook her food").

"Take something of your own, instead," Lex suggested. "Something to remind Alicia of you."

"I've just the thing." He opened a drawer half full of medals with their colored ribbon tags and tipped them out into the box. If there was any temptation to look through these decorations, marking the public highlights of his life, one more time before he buried them, he did not submit to it. "Alicia always laughed at these," he said. "She called them 'Glory Gongs'—and called me 'Highness' when I wore them."

"And now you're going to make her rest in peace with them forever and a day?"

"Why not? I always like to hear her laugh."

Lex arranged Mr. Busi's choices more evenly and pleasingly around the box and covered everything with packing straw, left over from his move from the villa to The Grove's ocean-side apartment, by way of a ten-month residence, at Joseph's expense, in the Bristol Pavilions, and a ten-month struggle with his conscience. "It's perfect actually. There couldn't be a better set of . . . votive offerings," she said. "A key. Two sorts of bell. The baubles of human pretension . . . excuse me, but you said as much yourself!"

Mr. Busi shook his head and smiled. He cannot take offense at her.

Mrs. Pencillon has no idea what we have planned. She wishes Mr. Busi all good fortune for the day and for the years ahead: "May they be plentiful." She has a gift for him, separate from Joseph's, an anthology of Mondazy's work with woodcuts and a silk page marker. Her inscription—she's clearly pleased with its daring—is their shared lyric from "The Pungent Rose": "I will obtain a kiss / Before she goes / That is my goal / Cajole her with the pungent rose / That's ready in my buttonhole / On nights like this." She still has spirit and she likes to tease. Mr. Busi blushes even and holds it up for me to read, his amanuensis, knowing I am party to its meaning.

Terina has perked up. Seeing Alfred blush is evidently gratifying. Now she is regretful that she is not well enough to join us on our picnic. "You'll not miss much," my neighbor promises. He still intends, despite her gift, to keep this outing private, not least because the requiem that Lex has planned, with its pagan undertones and its theatricality, is not in the best of taste. But Lex herself is not at all embarrassed or aware. "Then you must come with us," she says, taking full command. "We can make you comfortable, I'm sure. You can't not come. It's your sister, after all." I half step forward to interrupt and save the day, and Mr. Busi makes a pained face; the needle breaks his skin again. But it is too late.

"You mean Alicia?"

"Of course Alicia." Without a pause for thought—so typical of her—Lex describes the scattering of ashes and the ceremony that will take place today in the forest and how there will be prayers and "sad rejoicings."

"Bring her to me," Terina says, suddenly alert, color spreading on her cheeks. We do not catch her meaning straightaway. She has to add, "My sister. Bring her here."

I go out through the courtyard to the car that Joseph has supplied for us and come back with the brass-and-rosewood presentation coffer in which Alicia has spent her afterlife.

"Let me hold her," Terina says. She has to withdraw her hands from underneath the woolen throw on her knees and stop massaging her joints to take the container. She rests it on her lap and caresses the lid with its inlaid brass design—a bird in flight—until she cannot help but cry. She sits before us now in tears, although she has the grace—and perhaps the practice—to keep them silent. She cannot disguise the creasing and the thinning of her lips as she tries to muffle her sobs, however. She has to hold her fingers to her mouth and eyes; not salty tears, I think, but sweet and sorrowed ones, drawn from the darkness of the well.

This is when I ought to damn the protocols and disappoint my father yet again. I ought to reward her kindness with some kindness of my own and wrap the maharani in my arms. But, again, I am too slow to be warm. I cannot shift my legs. My limbs are frozen. It is Lex who has gone forward with a hug. Even Mr. Busi finds it in himself to step closer to his wife's sister and place a hand onto her shoulder stole, the fur. We all are murmuring, "Now now, there there, come come," those shortfall words of comfort. We must look and sound absurd to Joseph and his new fiancée, Marianne. They come onto the patio just in time to witness our embarrassed show of sympathy; "human forms" reaching out like some sculpted triad by Rodin, the shy man and the uncle and the crazy girl. Joseph, proudly sporting a new addition to his chin, a shaped camel beard but no mustache, cannot see his long-dead aunt perched like a box of chocolates on his mother's damaged knees.

*

I wish that I was feeling perkier for Mr. Busi's birthday trip, but I have not slept well. Certainly I have not slept for long. Friday night is when I look for entertainment in our town and stay out late. I try to be as charming as I can when Joseph introduces Marianne to us, but I can tell her fiancé is watching me as if he knows exactly why my eyelids seem so cumbersome; where I have been, with whom. It's obvious I am not liked. Perhaps it's simply that he cannot bear any men who are attentive to his mother. I have to say, though, that his Marianne seems a decent woman, keen to please and evidently more than fond of the man she'll marry in the coming spring. I should allow that if he's loved, then he is lovable—and must be admirable as well to those whom he lets close. But I am only fearful of him and his gimlet eyes, made all the more disturbing, strangely, by the beard. I wonder, when I take her hand in mine, if there is a way to press a warning on her palm, tap out in finger Morse perhaps an SOS. But I can tell by how she looks at me—at all of us, apart from Mrs. Pencillon—that she has been warned already, by Joseph. Watch out for them—especially the woman—he will have said. They're Uncle Alfred's hangers-on; he has become their private fool.

The truth is that Mr. Busi does seem rather coltish in our company, as if he feels obliged, as many *fathers* do, to lop off thirty years or more when Lex or anybody young, except me, is in the room. She tells him frequently how good he is for seventy, how spirited, how well, how open to the latest fads. He plays along with her. But when he is alone—I know—he is a different man. The inner walls of our apartments are not thick. I live just a step or so away from him, across the corridor, the

exact same space and distance actually as that between the boy
at his piano practicing Dell'Ova's "Carnival Caprice" and his
father with his lifted shirt, awaiting the syringe. I can hear not
quite his every move but enough to know when he is bathing,
coughing, cooking, going to the toilet (too frequently, I'd say),
or opening a cupboard or a drawer. I can even hear him pecking
round his pair of little rooms, a man with not enough to do. And
I can see the lights beneath his apartment door. They go off early
nowadays. My neighbor's fleeing to his bed as soon as it is dark,
I think, though clearly he is not asleep till late. His bedsprings
tweet like starlings. They start their choruses again before I go
to work, and at the weekends might continue far into the morning. It seems he finds no reason to get up. Sometimes it is midday
before I hear him opening his blinds or talking to himself.

My habit is, when I am free to keep him company, to rap on
his door with my knuckles—he does not like the new electric
bell—and simply call out "Five!," as if I am a concert manager
counting down his cue. That gives him time to rise or dress or
shave, to make himself and his reception room presentable. It
gives him time as well, I have to say, to open up some windows
and renew the air. What is it with the elderly?

Mr. Busi used to play piano when I first arrived as his tenant.
I could hear him practicing each day, trying even—though without success—to find a lyric for his "Persian Bells," the wounded,
tinkling lament he started composing for Alicia the night of the
attack at the larder door but that became, as well, a keening for
the boy. But evidently someone in the rooms above complained,
or at least requested in a handwritten note pushed below his door
that he should play only in "working hours" and keep his foot
on the soft pedal. "If you can hear it, so can we," they wrote. So

he closed the fallboard on his instrument and sat in silence in his room. "Some melodies are never meant to find their words," he says. It is the saddest phrase.

But when I come across and sit with him, he brightens up. His room is peopled once again. He'll even run his fingers up and down his keyboard—soft pedal down, of course—to reminisce about the concerts he has given and the standing he once had. Apart from that one haunting and chaotic week of bites and beatings, he's had a lucky life, there's no denying it, but no amount of luck prepares you for the loneliness of age, he says. "You're all I have," he adds disturbingly. I hardly dare to look at him. "And Lex, of course."

"And Mrs. Pencillon?"

"Well, yes."

My way of cheering him has been to jolt him out of talking only of the past and about himself and to make him listen to what is going on right now in our fast-changing and exhilarating town. He hardly leaves the apartment nowadays, except to visit Mrs. Pencillon, and so I am his ears and eyes and nose. If Nephew Joseph thinks he can guess why my eyelids seem so cumbersome this morning, then Mr. Busi truly knows, if he's been listening. I share with him what I have done on Friday nights, or most of it. Each week, it's something different, some fresh experience. In towns like ours—it's what we love—we can choose our company or choose to stay anonymous and still *belong*, whatever we prefer. I sample bars and clubs for him, I visit what is new or old, what's coming down, what's going up, what makes a city of our town, where we have pressed our foreheads on the world and what we've had to turn our backs against, the yeast and dough of daily life.

This morning, in the hour before Lex arrived to make her mad arrangements for the day and hunt for offerings, the two of us sat where we often sit on Saturdays, on Mr. Busi's duet stool close to the window and the light. "This is how I wasted my Friday evening and night," I told him, knowing that the strange and final episode of my adventures would unnerve him, as it has unsettled me. "First," I said, counting off the evening's events on my fingers, starting at my thumb, "I sat up on a shoeshine rostrum on the harborfront and watched the sailors and the deckmen come ashore, smelling of salted fish and tar, while my navy-blue oxfords were made as good as new by one of those sweet urchin boys. Yes, I tipped him. Royally. Well, like a minor prince, let's say.

"Then"—my index finger now—"I walked along the boulevard toward the old town, feeling spick and looking like a gentleman. And smelling good, as well—a mix of petrol and beeswax from the shoe polish. Well, let me tell you, I deserved an aperitif and appetizers, it's been a testing week, and so I spent an hour on the terrace of a bar, looked after by a waiter I have come to know by name. Maurice. What did I drink and eat? Those little cheese-and-chestnut pastries with some muscat de maquis.

"Then, part three of my adventures on the town"—my middle finger—"there was a poster for a boxing tournament pasted on the fencing to that building they are putting up, replacing the old butchers' hall. 'Trained Hospital Nurses Will Be in Attendance,' it promised, an enticement rather than a warning, I would say. I had to see that for myself. What are we humans if not curious, in both senses of the word? And so I took myself along and watched the adolescents in their shorts hurt each other for a silver cup and a week of bruises.

"I finished up"—my ring finger—"at midnight in another pothouse, drinking naval beer, where there were singers, dancers too, and people with opinions raging to be listened to, and faces that were crazed and beautiful and young. What then, what then? What isn't there? Our town is at its best at night. There's nothing that can't happen when it's dark. But you know that, Mr. Busi. You know that more than anyone."

He nodded his agreement: yes, he'd been a wild man on the town himself, at my age, and indeed the oddest things had happened to him in moonlight and under stars.

"But there is something unexplained," I told him finally, as we sat and shared the sunlight spreading on the sea beyond his window and the sandy beach, a portent for a dry birthday. I held up my right hand, palm toward my face, and wrapped my left hand round the little finger. "This is the pinkie of my night," I said. "When I went out last evening, I left—don't laugh—I left out two bananas on the countertop together with some other groceries. I meant to eat them later. My lonely midnight feast. Bananas can be sobering and help with sleep. It's the potassium, I believe. Or maybe just the sugar. But when I got home, a little drunk, I will admit, I found their skins tossed on the mat, discarded like a dirty pair of yellow socks. The mat was twisted round and bunched up on itself as if something or someone had got tangled up in it. My window was half open and the chair out on the deck had toppled on its side. There was a pungent smell as well, not actually a dreadful smell, but lingering." (Here I could not help but echo some phrases I'd heard Mr. Busi use to describe his own strange encounter at the larder door.) "It was neither sweet nor savory, but, well, let's say earthy, more like starch and mold." I sniffed as if to summon back the smell and check that

I had described it well, and nodded then, because I'd told the truth.

Now Mr. Busi tilted his face at me, his mouth parted by a question that he did not ask. He was not sure, I think, if I was being honest or just teasing him. "Potato peel," he muttered to himself but loud enough for me to hear, and shook his head.

"So that's the tale of my adventures on the town," I said, wagging my pinkie at him playfully, "and what I found when I returned, as told in fingers, both yellow ones and pink. What should we make of it?"

We sat in silence then, amused by making sense of what had happened in the night to those two missing fruits. "Some things are inexplicable," I said eventually, and laughed, because a thousand times before I've argued that they aren't, that all there is, is what's explained and what is left to be explained. No fathoms are beyond our reach, has always been my view. *Our* view. For both of us are rational by nature. We take comfort only from the matter of the universe, from body, substance, stuff.

"Perhaps the bosk, or what few shreds remain of it, is not as lifeless as we thought," Mr. Busi replied. "Don't tell my nephew, though. He'll come round with his gun."

12

As IT HAPPENS, I have already seen Joseph Pencillon with a shotgun on his arm, though I have been reluctant to admit as much to Mr. Busi, to tell him how I played a tiny part in making the bosk he loved and explored as a child the lifeless place it is today. That was the night four years ago, or five, when Soubriquet was nearly killed. It could be said, he brought the shooting on himself, by conducting a private vendetta in the public pages of *Indices* (now sadly closed, for lack of advertising revenue).

There had, of course, been a widespread tremor of anxiety when *The Register* finally published plans and details of The Grove. Townspeople wanted to be certain that our losses would be less than our gains. Two sets of slogans—FAMILIES, NOT FORESTRY and ROOFTOPS BEFORE TREETOPS; and SAVE THE LUNG—summarize the level of debate. Soubriquet was appointed, by himself, as Lord Protector of the Lung. "If Victor Hugo were alive and came to visit us again, he would be disappointed to discover how wheezy we've become for lack of oxygen, which, as any schoolchild knows, is gifted to us by the plants and trees," he wrote. "We used to be his 'City of Four Lungs'; quite soon, unless we call a halt on this so-called Grove, we'll be the city of only 'Three,' the people who forgot their duties and their legacy."

Soubriquet's dislike for Trader Pencillon had not abated since the night of, let us call it, *Cedric*'s debut in the gardens. He was careful, though, not to name "the timber man" in his columns and reports, though that tag was surely clue enough. To be believed, a journalist should seem reasoned and not personal. However, Soubriquet could not forget the fracas in the marquee on the night that *Mister Al* went off the map, the punches thrown, and his humiliation at the pretty knees of Katerine Pencillon.

She had hurried off that evening, as soon as *Cedric* had completed the first half of his impromptu concert, and so had not given Soubriquet a chance to right himself. He'd spent the hour after the interval fixated on her empty seat, convinced he was to blame for her early departure—her flight, in fact—although the only words he'd spoken to her, then or since, were innocuous, professional: "I'd love an interview." That was a phrase he'd used a thousand times, and not always with hopes of a seduction. Still, it was clear he'd made her feel uncomfortable and then she'd left the marquee in a dreadful flap.

Soubriquet could not help but link these two events and want to—no, not make amends but save his face. He'd had to go back to his dreary apartment and his ungrateful cat in the blackest of moods, greatly darkened by an odd event on his way home. In the shadow of the town hall, in an alleyway that leads up to the boulevards and bars, a man had come up from behind, walloped Soubriquet across the skull with something not as hard as stone or glass, or timber even, and then run on ahead. It really didn't even hurt, though it had been a shock and an assault, mainly on his self-esteem. The perpetrator was young and poor, a street kid. He'd evidently—from the skip in his run—seen the offense as a jape, a paying dare, funded probably by Pencillon: "I'm hiring you to clout that fellow but not so badly that he'll call the police." Soubriquet had played the details through his head too many times since the concert. Now, with The Grove, he could revenge himself. He'd do what he could to stop that tycoon and his building schemes, while seeming to be only the Noble Savior of the Bosk.

It was an uphill struggle, though. Many of his articles were spiked or devitalized. His editor could not allow his weekly magazine to make too many enemies among the very class who were its influential readers or its investors. The Grove could not be attacked politically or as evidence of even more disparities between the ways in which the poor were treated in our town and how the prosperous were sheltered and defended. The architects could not be pilloried for providing for only the rich and the powerful; no town will flourish if it does not welcome wealth or privilege, nor will any magazine.

What was allowed were Soubriquet's defenses of the plants and animals with which we all had lived so closely "since our market stone was raised in 1382." There'd always been a thick and scrubby forest on our doorsteps, on the rocky headland to the east of the town, he lectured his readers. Some of the tallest trees within the bosk were older than our oldest citizen and could expect to live another hundred years. "Look at the plans and at the deceiving models they have made," he typed on his new Underwood, with its endorsing carriage bell and letter *o*, his trousers loosened for the kill, "and you will see our once impenetrable town forest reduced to decorative crescents of vegetation, as lifeless, tamed, and managed as a pot of mint or bay on a kitchen veranda."

The developers owed it to the town that funded them and to botany itself, he said, to save what trees and plants they could. There should be no felling or razing to the ground, but rather a regime of rescue and conservation. Some trees—the rarest ones, the oldest ones, the grandest ones—must remain "exactly where they are" and surrounded by enough open ground for their roots to flourish with sufficient rain. The projected villas and apartments of The Grove could not expect simply to kill the land; they'd have to dig their trenches and sink their pipework somewhere else. NATURE BEFORE PLUMBING was (he judged) his witty slogan.

Many of the smaller indigenous shrubs, Soubriquet suggested, should be dug up, not cut down, and transported with their entire roots wrapped in hessian to be replanted where they could "continue giving pleasure"—in the Mendicant Gardens, for example. What plants had once flourished there had been pretty much destroyed of late, he reported, by the homeless poor, who'd either used the branches for firewood or boiled the leaves for dinner. Clear the Gardens of their human inhabitants, he advised, shamefacedly but cunningly, he thought. But provide them with some comfortable alternatives: "I'm sure The Grove will want to set aside some land for hostels to be built." Then they could replant the shrubs and smaller trees, and every home dweller in those less wealthy districts would benefit from an open, cultivated park to walk around in, despite the disappearance of the bosk.

What Soubriquet did not say, of course, was that his Defense of Nature would cost the developers—Pencillon included—a lot of time and money. He could imagine a great line of carts queu-

ing at the fringes of the bosk as workers dug into the ground
to Save the Trees. He could imagine Trader Pencillon watching
from his flashy car as, plant by plant, as shrub by shrub, his profits were reduced. Yes, Soubriquet with Victor Hugo at his side
had made a nuisance of himself, just as he'd hoped.

Joseph Pencillon was not a man to be defeated by a cogent
argument. He treated Soubriquet's editor to lunch and managed,
by the end of it, to make an offer no one would refuse. "You will
need, though, to give my magazine a reason to . . ." The editor
did not like to say *retreat.* "Accommodate," the timber merchant
suggested; it was the perfect word, for his new ally in the vulnerable world of magazines would go home that day with the promise of a pied-à-terre in town "at cost"; though, come to think
of it, he wasn't sure if he'd been fooled—"at cost" might mean
exactly what it said, no discount or concession. Pencillon, however, while eating his lunch chops, had come up with an easy way
to call Soubriquet's bluff and save the editor's face.

That Saturday, in an article not attributed to Soubriquet,
Indices reported on the plan "of a respected businessman and
developer" to replant the Mendicant Gardens "exactly as suggested in these pages in last week's edition" and return them to
the leafy splendors they had once enjoyed. The grounds would
be secured by day and night against the homeless and the damage they had already caused. "The benefits of this are clear," the
editor's accomplice wrote. "Even Monsieur Hugo would approve
of this resuscitation of a lung. A toxic part of town, where, of
late, it has been too dangerous to stray, will once again be attrac-
tive to visitors and our more respectable townspeople. Its neighborhoods will benefit as well from their proximity to this new
public amenity."

Restocking the Gardens "with little plants" would be easy and inexpensive but would appear charitable, Joseph explained to his colleagues and his partners at their weekly conclave in his first-floor offices in town. "What could it take? Three vans, four men, five days, at the most?" But their plans for The Grove would not be changed, not by a single twig. The buildings had priority. There'd be no paupers' hostels, certainly. The meeting room was full of men chortling at the very thought. And, of course, the trees of what had once been called the bosk would have to go. They shouldn't save a single one. A chainsaw, zip-zeep, zip-zeep; they were down. Let's not waste our sensibilities on them, he said. Their timber would be used for roof frames and for windows. That was the only continuity he could promise to "the lung lovers."

But even this was not enough. Joseph planned to outwit Soubriquet in other, inexpensive ways. "Most people of this town really will not shed a tear for trees," he explained. "But they will always want to save an animal. It should be Wildlife before Plumbing, shouldn't it? Nobody truly cares about the plants." His proposal was that Pencillon and Co. would act as Noah and his Ark and round up "all the living beasts" out in the bosk for relocation somewhere more secure.

"Ship them out to Poverty Park?" someone suggested.

"Exactly so. The perfect place." Joseph had to smile to himself. He'd go down in history as the man who'd saved the animals. "We'll have a festival," he continued. "A weekend set aside. We'll ask for volunteers. Free labor is the best. Their kids can come. I'll lay on vans and food. Imagine it, before we start to build, before we even clear the ground, we form a great long line with gongs and nets and drive the creatures into pens, enough to satisfy the press at least. Anything too dangerous I'll shoot. I'm glad to play a modest part. I have had a rifle loaded and ready for just such a circumstance. The rest can go out to the Park, where they belong. It'll cost us hardly anything, either in money or in time. But, gentlemen . . ." He spread his hands to invite his colleagues to complete his sentence and laughed out loud to hear them say, "We will be the defenders of the town," "philanthropists," "civic champions," and "the good Samaritans."

"*Pro bono publico*," he said, hoping to impress them even more and thinking too that possibly that empty bay in the Avenue of Fame was now more securely his.

So it was that one weekend in the September following Mr. Busi's elevation to the Avenue of Fame, Noah's Ark put ashore in our town just after dawn in the form of twenty or so motorized trucks and vans and several hundred joyful volunteers. I blush to admit I was among the students there who came to make a din and maybe see some of the creatures that up till then we'd only heard or read about. Why would I participate? Just curiosity, I think, and youthful innocence. I'd no idea this escapade would change the nature of our town for good. Many of us were not sober and none of us was rested. We'd passed the evening in the late bars and then spent the night in the early cafés, where, for a price, our coffee could be laced with alcohol. We had been asked to come equipped with stout shoes and gloves, thick trousers—for there were snakes and rodents to ensnare and thorns to avoid—and something metal to bash and bang.

At dawn, and full of drink and high spirits, we made our way along the promenade, helping ourselves to anything that might make a noise if struck. The lids of rubbish bins were perfect for the task, and so were the enamel advertising signs that many shops and restaurants had swinging from chains. With a tug from several sturdy arms, they would snap free. I am ashamed to say I stole a distilling kettle and a spigot wrench from the deck of a parked delivery truck, telling myself that I would put them back on my way home. My father would have been turning in his grave, had he been dead. We walked along the seafront, banging what we had, not caring for the residents or sleepers on the beach, but hoping to shake the town awake. We wanted everyone to come to see the animals and take part in what could be the best adventure of their lives.

I had never been this far along the promenade before, so Mr. Busi's villa and the Pastry House were unknown to me. If I'd had the gift of seeing into the future, I might have studied them more closely, paid more attention to the surviving older buildings in the space where eventually I'd live myself, as Mr. Busi's obliging tenant at the meeting of the ocean and The Grove. But actually I do not think I noticed them at all, although, for sure, had I bothered to look up into the bedrooms behind the balcony, I might have spotted my landlord peering out, twitching at his curtains. He says he does remember being woken up. The sound of bin lids often woke him up, of course. But on this occasion the cause was not animal and innocent, but human and ferocious. Afterward, after we had finished with our kettles and our wrenches, all the beings that had once dined in his yard on his kitchen waste would have been driven out or captured, stunned and then removed. Mr. Busi could not say—and still he cannot say—if this was an event that wrecked and ruined him beyond repair, but he is sure that what took place that morning proved enough to drive him from his home, to taint his love for it. He'd lost his natural habitat, along with all the other creatures of the bosk. By lunchtime that day he had signed the documents that let the family villa go.

What I remember is the looming presence of the trees, back-lit by the ascending day, and—something I had heard but never feared before and know that I will never hear again in that same place—the shingled menace of the tide.

We waited at the assembly point, a paved square with formal gardens and benches, until our group had swollen to a hundred or more, all beating on our metal pieces, the most discordant orchestra. It was enjoyable. We felt like kids. Among us were faces not unknown to me: some lecturers, a cousin whom I hadn't seen for years, a group I recognized from bars, but Sou-briquet had to be pointed out to me. I knew his work, of course. I'd followed everything he'd written about The Grove. He was much older than I expected, and shabbier. He stood out from the crowd: his anger was unmissable; so was the fact that he was either drugged or drunk, more so than me or any of my friends. His face, caught by the early light, was green on gray, or "mold on slate," as he would say when we met by chance at the shoe-shine podiums only last year and he recounted bitterly what he could remember of his days as "a lung lover."

What I know now, but had no inkling of that morning of the evictions, was that he had been sacked the previous afternoon. "It was a matter of principle," he would claim. "The indepen-dence of a magazine should never be for sale. I handed them an ultimatum and they buckled under it." But I suspect the ultima-tum was the editor's, not his. The choice was either retaining a troublesome employee or obtaining a cosy pied-à-terre. Sou-briquet must have known that, and he must have known as well who had plotted his dismissal. Why else would he have turned up that night to volunteer for Joseph's "relocations" (dislocations might have been a truer term) if he didn't mean to corner the man he had good cause to loathe and create a scene, a rematch of the scuffle in the marquee?

It was hard work, wading through the undergrowth. It took an hour just to reach the outcrops at the top. The morning chill, the salty breeze, the lifting light, the effort of the climb into the bosk—all this sobered us. We soon grew bored and impatient. I don't remember spotting anything much bigger than a hog, or any creature rarer than a dove, or any beast more dangerous than my own companions in the hunt, and Soubriquet, of course. The drama, so we heard, was at the far end of the beatings, where the flocks and packs and herds and swarms of flushed-out animals were running into traps or pens or flying into nets. The best tasks of the night, so it's been claimed, were bringing down the large and panicked stags with lariats and then hobbling them with twine, or catching hold of snakes with foundry gloves. The worst were handling the Mustelidae, which could protect themselves with noxious and offensive sprays. There were some claims that naked humans had been seen and caught, and other claims of unnamed, unknown beasts, new to science, of mythical, unlikely creatures, those necessary monsters of our dreams against which we have to bolt our doors at night, of giant rats the size of sheep, of monkeys with the upright gait of men, of slug bunnies, of bush-lopers with tacky hands and sticky tongues.

There was a rumor too, a rumor that proved to be as true as it was brutal, that under the cover of the beaten metal and the mayhem in the scrub and woods, other vans with soldiers at their wheels or policemen out of uniform searched our boulevards and alleyways for any mendicants who dared to show their grubby faces or tried to go back to their flimsy homes inside the Gardens once the dawn had come. Any screams were drowned out by the animals and by us, the drunken volunteers. This was never spoken of out loud and not reported either, but I've heard whispered stories ever since, about the rounding up and splitting up of families, of constables seen tossing children into open trucks, of beggars never being seen again on corners where they had once been a fixture, of casual loafers who looked down-at-heel or simply indigent being pulled away like criminals, of slappings, kickings, broken bones, of sleeping bodies in their bedrolls being dragged along the alleyways like animals to slaughter.

I cannot claim I saw the evidence myself. There might be philanthropic explanations that we do not know about, but one thing is certain: once the animals had gone, our town seemed suddenly swept clean of shabby people and the needy poor as well. For quite a few months afterward, nobody asked for money on the street or had to eat from bins. The boulevards were better dressed and better fed, less boisterous and wild, less anxious and ashamed. And no one ever set up home again in the Mendicant Gardens among the newly planted beds or even tried to. Its residents had disappeared and taken all their edginess along with them. Our "vagabonds and scroungers" ended up—depending on the teller—on a cargo boat bound for Ellis Island in New York, or shot dead and used as scarecrows, hanging from the branches of trees too far from town for anyone to know or care, or working in a mine somewhere, as slaves, or as corpses buried in a common grave, or as bobbing bodies in the sea, for fishermen to catch and throw back to the fish as bait, or with the animals as castaways in Poverty Park. Who knows? Our town will never be the same again, though it is hard for anyone to say if this is for the better or the worse. Each gain is paid for with a loss.

Of one thing I am certain, though, because I witnessed it. The incident that everyone would talk about quite openly and with malicious glee occurred that morning not in the Gardens but in the bosk. We had gone forward through the trees and undergrowth in a line. I think every one of us was bleeding from the hands or face or had ripped his sleeves. And we were itching from the ticks that, once they got beneath our clothes, favored armpits, kneepits, and groins. It was a great relief to come out at the summit of the bosk, where there were rocks and open ground, with panoramic views across the ocean and the town, and where the Grove developers had set up their first-aid tent and a canteen with hot drinks and croque madames topped by lukewarm béchamel. Joseph never fails to oversell himself. I was waiting for the disinfectant and the salve for the gashes on my cheek—I cannot help but think of Mr. Busi and Katerine now—when Mr. Pencillon himself arrived. He had been lent an army general-purpose car, without glass windows or a roof, to force a way through foliage, and he was dressed to fit the part. He had fatigues in olive drab; he had a hunting rifle on his arm; he had a look of triumph on his face. The night had gone extremely well. He'd come to make a humble speech of thanks. We should not think we'd shed our blood or spoiled our clothes for something not worthwhile.

Joseph stood up in the front well of his vehicle and called for our attention, but it wasn't him that we were looking at for long. Soubriquet had stepped up to the fender of the car and was leaning on its bonnet, looking like he planned on lifting it and tipping out its driver. His face was just as green on gray as it had been down on the promenade. Somehow he hadn't sobered up, despite the damp, despite the morning cold, despite the effort of the climb. I couldn't catch his every word. Much of what he shouted out was garbled anyway. He wasn't missing vowels but consonants. The man was making a spectacle of himself in front of the "stinking" Pencillon. We were embarrassed, though not sure if we ought to intervene: stop him now and we might lose half of a lively anecdote; pull the man away, and he might turn his anger onto us. But it was Pencillon himself who brought the drama to an end. When Soubriquet began to rock the vehicle, his rival lifted up his gun and pointed it at his head. "Let's see if there's a brain in there, Neanderthal," he said. I will not report what Soubriquet offered in return, but let's just say it was surprising from a man who until that day had earned his living deploying words with elegance and focus. The next thing that we heard was a crack of detonation and a bullet spinning through the air.

*

I have to hand it to the timber merchant. He has to be a superb shot, although we didn't know that straightaway. Soubriquet was bucking on the ground like a badly slaughtered hog. You should have heard the row he made. We half expected him to be clean dead and only moving, like a headless eel, because his body's muscles were convulsing and in spasm. We also half expected him to have survived but with a bloody tunnel through his skull. But actually we—or, that's to say, the nurses from the first-aid tent—could not find a mark on him. He was, it's true, not hearing well and he was trembling from shock. He might have wet himself, but no one's sure. Somebody said that Pencillon had only shot a blank, but others claimed to see the bullet whiz—a tiny comet with a silver tail, not fiery as you might imagine—and heard it strike and bury itself into one of the bosk's ill-fated trees. Joseph had sent the bullet just a fingerbreadth away from his opponent's ear. Somewhere in one of those fine mansions in The Grove, perhaps, there is a doorframe or a beam that has a bullet at its heart.

I guess we should not be surprised that the shooting in the bosk, like the clearing of the Gardens, was not reported in our press (though word of it, I have heard, put the lid on Joseph's hopes of being mayor). The incident was too sensational for *The Register*, and *Indices* was already compromised. Its report the weekend after struck a flat and measured note. I cut it out and kept the piece as a record of the tiny part I'd played. I have it still in my back rooms across the corridor from Mr. Busi.

"The throng of animals," it read, "which have for far too long, against their natures, had to forage for their daily sustenance in restaurant yards and at our waste bins, have finally been liberated. In a coordinated weekend of clearance and capture organized by our leading civic bodies and funded entirely by the developers and the builders of the forthcoming Grove, up to a thousand volunteers, comprising mostly students from the College and Academy as well as neighborhood groups keen to make their pets and children safe, gathered at six assembly points on the fringes of the town's old bosk and drove the captives therein to a better, truer life beyond.

"A multitude of mostly pigs and deer, together with wild dogs and cats and some few rarer creatures, were transported in vehicles out to Poverty Park, where there is natural nourishment and where their lives will be less confined. Others completed their journeys to the forests under their own power, so to speak, either by wing or by wind. There they can exist, self-possessed, in harmony and numb to any knowing fear of death or passing time but liberated—unlike us of greater consciousness but more domestic passions—from the nagging bells and gongs of city life; a kind of simple paradise and one, perhaps, we might regard as preferable to our own small and stifling existences.

"Readers will not be dismayed to learn that snakes and rats were not afforded civic transport to this Eden but were more swiftly dispatched to another Promised Land, the Province of Eternal Hibernation. After the relocations were completed, Joseph Pencillon, speaking on behalf of The Grove Development Group, expressed his relief that 'his town' (Mr. Pencillon announced his mayoral candidacy at the beginning of the month) has finally been freed of 'all its brutes and beasts.' 'We can safely roam our streets at night without fear of animals, clothed or otherwise,' he said."

There was a further paragraph, added by the editor himself: "Our town council has advised that residents, wishing to avoid future infestations of unwelcome animals in or near their properties, should take greater care with disposing of uneaten food and meal waste. Domestic bins should be regularly doused in strong disinfectant, and edible scraps should be splashed with bleach or poison." All he needed now were the illustrations for the page, some print blocks from the magazine's archives, ready for re-use. That was the final time that Alfred Busi's face appeared in *Indices*. The caption read THE RECENT ELDER VICTIM OF AN ANIMAL ATTACK, but did not give the bandaged face a name.

13

THAT BANDAGED FACE WAS restored to almost new within
a month of those two attacks—in the Gardens and at the larder
door—six years ago. But he has not recovered yet, my neighbor says. That week of kicks and scratches changed his life, both
for the better and the worse. He has a flat scar on his upper lip
to show for it. And his dread of rabies, or at least needles, has
remained. Although Mr. Busi cannot pretend to regret refusing
the full ten injections of antiserum and enduring only one, he still
to this day has nightmares about the virus coming back to finish him off. Too often he has read in Alicia's *Home Encyclopedia
of Health and Conduct*—a nagging presence on his bookshelf—
that rabies can lie dormant for several months and even years
and then, restored by sleep, emerge in its most aggressive form,
amplifying in the body too speedily for victims "to bid farewell."
The insomnia and occasional headaches that he still suffers from,
as well as the shivers and the sweats and the general sense of
weakness that afflict most people of his age, might yet be taken
as symptoms that could place him just a hydrophobic week away
from death. He is still faintly anxious whenever he turns on a tap.
He wonders if he's running out of days.

"Do I look old?" he asked this morning as we set off to visit the Pencillons, not wanting us to speak the truth.

"Is this your fiftieth?" Lex inquired, and he was pleased.

And then he turned to me. "You're not bad for seventy," I said, not wanting to seem false. But I could tell this was not an answer he desired. Being not bad for your age is a validation of a kind, I suppose, but not the endorsement or the reassurance anyone might seek on reaching seventy. I should have said, "You are not old."

I wondered if I had upset him in some wider sense, because in the car that Joseph has provided he was silent, even when Lex jumped in and, for the third time this morning, kissed him, like a daughter, on his forehead. Then I remembered what had been said to him as we descended in the apartment building's new-fangled lift with its reluctant gate, which his stiff hands could not quite shut without my help. A couple of other owners, two women from the upper floor, possibly the ones who requested that he play piano quietly, were already in the lift. Seeing their neighbor dressed up for the day in his picnic clothes and with his vintage walking stick, one of them said, "You're looking jaunty today." Mr. Busi had both smiled and winced. Of course, he hated words like that, like *jaunty*, or *trim*, or *dapper*. They applied only to men who were too old to count, not to a famous singer, now retired but celebrated in the Avenue of Fame. They made him feel less manly, a person of little value or stature. If I could have read at the time the pained expression on his face when he heard *jaunty*, I would have had him say to them, "This stick, this cudgel in my hand, drew blood. I'm not too old to draw some blood again. I'm not too old to play piano loudly."

Perhaps it's just as well that Mrs. Pencillon has come with

us today; at least Mr. Busi will not feel the oldest there, despite his age. How could she not come? How could she let her sister's ashes fly and not be there to raise a hand with her farewells? How could we leave her sitting in that wicker chair, unattended and in tears? We had to help her down the courtyard paths into the street. She even took my arm and let me bear her modest weight. But now that she is settled in a throne of cushions in the front seat of the car, next to Albert, the driver Joseph has hired to spend his day with us, her mood has changed again. She's happy to look out—as are we all—at our ancient, changing town, its spires and castellations now overshadowed by squarer blocks, its pavements slightly narrower to accommodate more cars and trams, its street-level windows on the sea reduced from when I was a boy, its gradual loss of trees, its new rapidity. The business and the bustle have increased, of course. I would not cross the boulevards these days without a two-way check, and then a hesitation. "Look twice, pause twice, pray twice, then dash," is what they say. But still I love my town and how it proudly holds its own between the ocean and the sky, despite the improvements and refinements coming out of town hall.

Once we have left the outskirts and reached the region's highest point, at Buttress Hill, Albert parks beside the road, so that he—and either of us men—can put the bushes to good use and then study the landscape at its best without having to bang our foreheads and our noses against the window of the motorcar.

This is the backbone of our land, where, even on clear days, according to the guidebooks, you can spin around through a full circle and "not see a single chimney pot." I spin around, as I have done in this same spot a dozen times before, my arms held out, my fingers spread to catch the solstice wind, and do not see a single chimney pot. To our left, the south, we blink into the sun to view the headlands and the distant bays, the sand beds, kelp swards, boulder chokes, Fort Island with its light tower, shimmering in the heat, the moorings and the boats, and then, as far as any human eye can see, diminishing and paling in the offing, islets, shale banks, channel reefs.

Today there is a liner in the harbor, the steamship *Red Cadiz*, a frequent visitor. A cargo boat is in the offing, sitting high with empty holds. To the north, we see a scrubby version of the bosk, though thinner on the ground, and dry, its wind-hunched saline elms just surviving all the hardships of the hills. Ahead, the timeless west of farmyards, orchards, cropping fields, paddocks, pasturelands, and meadows stretches hopefully, until the soil becomes too thin or stony for its plows. There the ancient forests still remain, the old tall world of undergrowth and canopies. We can make out the gray-green mist of distant trees and Poverty Park, although we are still half an hour's drive away.

The hawks are flat-winged this morning, biding their time high above Buttress Hill. We crane our necks to watch, but nothing can diminish their remoteness or reduce their deep indifference to us. They are aloof and neither friend nor foe, but unforthcoming, and uninvolved. A hawk is not a joyful sight. Then we are blessed, befriended even. Swifts descend. A rare event. They have been brought close to the ground by the flies and bugs we have disturbed with our scuffing and our car. They are, indeed, as close as gnats, nearer to our heads as any bat or starling would ever dare to come. All too briefly, we are bombarded by their every duck and dive, their yachting wings, their eerie and falsetto screams, but, in moments, they have taken what they can and are aloft again, higher than the hawks, mere specks. Yet they have lifted us and blessed our outing. They are a thrilling bird. They bring good fortune, it is said. We feel a little sanctified by them and full of hope. Mr. Busi's birthday trip is starting on a cheery note.

Mr. Busi, though, is quiet and thoughtful as we travel on. Having his sister-in-law in the car as well as Albert, a stranger to us all, seems to have dampened his spirits, despite the swifts. Terina and the driver are our parents for the day, sitting at the front, blocking our view ahead like adults at the cinema. We three in the rear are silenced by the purring of the car. I cannot help but recollect what Mr. Busi has told me of the Saturdays he spent as a young boy with the Kleins, making this same journey, except in that case the adults at the cinema were the pastry man himself and fat Honik, the dog. In those days only the roads out of town were surfaced and smooth, but after Buttress Hill, where the farmlands were reached, the ridgeway track became rutted and uneven. The boys had bounced around among the buns and bagels, amid the overwhelming smell of yeast and cakes—what was the phrase he used?—like "overbaked bread rolls." Bread rolls that bounced? That seems a thousand years ago, in magic times, the sort of animated rolls that Mr. Disney might invent, with faces cut into the dough, and crusty hair, and cocktail sticks as legs. The boys would clash their heads and tumble-scream at every pothole on the way, like cartoon clowns, enjoying their discomfort.

But we are cosseted and cushioned. The car's a sitting room on wheels. You might close your eyes and never know that you were traveling. Even the forest track into the Park that Mr. Busi has described as punishing is now a leveled, surfaced way, wide enough for tourist coaches to drive along when it is dry. The clearings themselves, where we must park, have not changed much, he says, as we get stiffly from the car at last and stretch ourselves, but they look tamed and managed now and, as ever these days, there is paper litter everywhere, so what you take at first to be an unusual leaf or some wild bloom is just an empty packet of cigars, a scrap of magazine or orange peel. There are barbecue braziers, picnic benches roughly made out of fallen timber, salt licks for the deer and ungulates, overflowing oil cans, supposedly too tall for animals, cemented into the ground for picnickers' litter and waste, knotted ropes to help any children scale the branches. And there are botanic labels on many of the trees and shrubs as well as a fraying "Key to the Flowers," meant to help us to identify the scented brushwood, the heliotropes and asphodels, the cistuses and genistas, as well as the less pretentious day docks and viper weeds. There is, as well, a raised and dated plaque to mark "The Release Site" of more than fifteen hundred animals, rescued from the confines of the town and then set free—many with numbered and colored identity tags. This was, it adds, "a public initiative, supported by . . ." Joseph's is the third name on the list.

Albert has driven as close as possible to a relatively clean and grassy bay, but there is broken ground and undergrowth between his car and the tables and benches we have chosen for our picnic. It is my job to take the cushions and the blankets from the front seat and make the picnic comfortable for Mrs. Pencillon. Lex and Mr. Busi, with his walking stick, his famous clouting stick, tucked for the moment under his arm, are doing their best to help his sister-in-law through the tangle in their way, the rough-strewn ground, and not making a good job of it. Albert comes to them from behind and simply picks her up as if she is as light

as balsa wood or some skimpy child. She's just a little shocked,
I think—when was the last time Katerine Pencillon was hoisted
by a man?—but laughing nevertheless with embarrassment and
girlish joy. Some women's voices can stay young. I think the two
of them have had a chance to break the ice in their front seats and
now are almost friends. She is still *noticed*, after all. In moments
she is sitting like a queen—like a maharani, as I've said—on her
shaded throne of cushions. Now I must unload the car and carry
what we need—the hamper and the wooden produce box with
its offerings—across the open ground to where we mean to pass
the day. Mr. Busi himself takes charge of Alicia's coffer.

Albert does not mean to stay. It would embarrass him and
us. He claims to have a relative to visit, not so far away. But he is
vague about the place, so either he has a woman that he hopes to
meet, or he knows a bar where he can drink, or he is lying, dip-
lomatically. I'm sure he'd rather spend his time alone, snoozing
in the car at Joseph's expense, than being bored by us. He will
come back to "rescue" us, he promises, a little after dusk. We've
said we want to see the sun go down, the huge solstice sun; we
want to see the forest darken; we want to see the first star and the
moon.

We have the clearings to ourselves—tomorrow, Sunday, is
the busy day—but not for long. A little Italian car arrives with
hikers. And then a pair of weekend wives, with dogs. And then a
tourist coach. Some of the wealthy passengers from the *Red Cadiz*
have followed us in our mobile sitting room to see the forest creatures and then tick the Poverty Park box in their *Bohm & Hannë
Travel Guide*, before heading off to tick the other boxes at all the
other sites. We can tell exactly what they're reading as they pick
their way between the trees, their books open at identical pages.

We know as well whose face is shown in the guide, the wounded, bandaged victim of an "ape attack." Mr. Busi steps back into the shade, not responding if he's nodded at or greeted by any cruise passengers meaning only to be pleasant though not truly caring who he is. He's just an old man, in his summer clothes, and sitting with his own ménage—a wife, two adult children, they suppose—around a picnic table, the perfect, rounded, modern family. He's not the wild and naked creature they have hoped to see; he's not one of "the rarest *humans* in the world."

The rarest human in the world, the one that I would like to see myself if only to discredit it, the one that Mr. Busi has encountered twice, the last time in the company of Lex and Terina—could very well be close at hand, if he, if she, if it exists. Some of the tourists have clearly been convinced by what they've read or been told by the tour guides selling them their tickets: that there are indeed "humanzees" surviving in the forests. They have binoculars and cameras, and are tense with expectation. Those who want it will find evidence, no doubt, though nothing scientific to record. That coughing in the distance—that sneezing too—might very well be hominid. That fibrous scat, knobbly with seeds, is what you might expect from Neanderthals or squalid savages. That flat and sloshy footprint in the mud, so handily close to where the tourists left their bus, must surely be the mark of a standing ape. The pad of the heel and the splay of the toes, where the mire has welled up between them, are photographed by all the visitors. It will not occur to them that every day, just after dawn, a local lad in the pay of the tour guides comes to wet the ground with his own urine and then remove a shoe and sock to leave a single footprint in his splosh. The guides will be rewarded by gratuities.

Yet even I, for all my rationality, for all my certainty that everything that's true is intelligible and provable, cannot dismiss entirely what these tourists have come here to encounter for themselves, a "people" summoned from the past. There's what occurred to Mr. Busi at the villa's bins; there are the rumors from that dawn of animal evictions; there is the folklore (always based on something real); there is what happened—I mention this, though more than half in jest—to my bananas earlier today. I have the sense, though not the proof—the *sense* in non*sense*, probably—that something other than ourselves persists. Something wilder and more animated but still resembling us. Something that must scavenge on its naked haunches for roots and berries, nuts and leaves, roaches, maggots, frogs and carrion, stolen eggs and honey. Something that might yet lack "the Ten Markers of Humanity" that place us at the pinnacle of Nature: words and fire, tools and beads, wheels and clothing, laughter, love and shame, and of course an apprehension of mortality. I have to wonder, though, when we come tumbling down, our cities and our towns, as tumble down they must, when our apartments and our boulevards are tenanted by rats and weeds, who will survive? Not those of us who travel in cars like sitting rooms but those who scrap for morsels every day, and can find water just by smell, and have the gift of poverty.

*

Whatever mood he might have been in this morning and later at the Pencillons, Mr. Busi is now the best of hosts. He's singing, actually, though only to himself, as he shuffles through the rocky limestone terraces, looking, he explains, for a replacement talisman. He's lived for far too long without his lucky charm, his *Gryphaea*. He'll need another for the next decade. And he succeeds. He dislodges from the ground a decent heavy one, though not as fine as the fossil stolen from him in the Gardens, and pockets it. His good fortune can resume.

We have this picnic bay all to ourselves, despite the to and fro of two more tourist coaches and other independent visitors, which keep the clearings busy through the day. All of us, except Terina, who is cold no matter the temperature, have taken off our jackets and our shoes. Lex sits cross-legged in her full-sails-ahead skirts and smokes her dark-skinned cigarettes, quite happily. I sit on the picnic bench, at Terina's side, while Mr. Busi opens Joseph's picnic hamper and takes out the contents, one at a time, admiring each one—for Joseph's mother's sake—quite fulsomely. I help by chasing off the many flies that come to see what food there is. As you'd expect, there is too much. Joseph wants us to admire his generosity. And we do. "He has been kind and thoughtful," we reassure his mother; she evidently is embarrassed by his undue largesse. The cutlery is copper-burnished steel, better than what most people have at home. The champagne flutes are proper glass. The plates are Maison Marie Cosse and decorated—surely not for only his uncle's benefit—with the number 70 in seventy different fonts. The napkins too have Mr. Busi's age embroidered at their hems.

"Foie gras, from France," says Mr. Busi, placing a molded jar on the tabletop. "Green olives preserved in eau de Provence. And caviar, of course. Well, Russian salmon caviar, which is almost just as good and certainly less gray. What's this? I've absolutely no idea. Sportsman's Relish. And this? It says it's gorse coulis. Who ever heard of such a thing?" He holds it to his nose

and says, "It smells of coconut and peas." We are relieved—for
Terina's sake; her son has not intended to be mocked—when he
has finished with the jars and their exotic contents, and pulls free
some rustling packets of bread triangles, the closest we will get to
sandwiches. The bread in fact is orange-stained, a not unpleasant taste, and the fillings are uncommon. We can't decide on one
pâté. It could be fish; it could be something from Japan. And
there are desserts as well, with cakes and pastries, more than we
can eat. This is a picnic fit for kings and queens in the sculptured
gardens of some palace, but I cannot imagine anything less con-
gruous for this untidy clearing in the Park. "Perhaps we ought
to ask the next coachload of visitors to join us," Lex suggests.
Mr. Busi shakes his head. "I shouldn't worry, none of it will go
to waste," he says, and lifts his chin toward the forests. "Hunger
lives among those trees, according to the pastryman. What was
it Mr. Klein used to say, meaning both his clients in town and his
customers out here? Bake them cake and they will come."

We have a satisfying day, elated by champagne and spices,
although we are just slightly ill at ease, and too keen perhaps to
smile and stay polite rather than enjoy ourselves full-heartedly.
We know that what awaits us is a sort of funeral; at dusk, once we
have eaten and relaxed, we'll spread the ashes and inter the past
in its clumsy produce box. It would not do for us to be too frivo-
lous, nor would it do for us to be in any way combative, though
I detect impatience at the table, from the true adults. But there
must be no tension in the air while Alicia is waiting in her coffer, and listening—although she is not listening. That's just our
game, or Lex's anyhow. "Five at the table," she has said, meaning that the ashes are a living presence in a way. Lex even pours a
glass of champagne for her, the long-departed wife, and lifts it for

her when we come to toast our birthday celebrant. He's reached what easily could be his last decade, I think. We might soon be coming out to scatter him, the celebrated singer come to dust.

"Feel free to wander, if you want," Mr. Busi says, once we have pushed aside our plates, too full to make much headway with the cakes. "Terina and I are happy to take things easy for a while, but you two ought to make the most of it." And then I realize that the impatience I have sensed is his impatience with both Lex and me. He wants us to go off. So I do what I'm told and walk toward the trees, my shoulders down, as if I've been admonished like a child. Lex skips ahead, happy to be on the loose. There's something that my landlord needs to say to Mrs. Pencillon, of course, and not be heard by us, some truce he wants to offer her, some armistice that must be brokered at this table, on this day, with Alicia's coffer, still unopened, between the two of them. I do not think he means to discuss with her some quite mundane matter—his will, perhaps, Joseph's disinheritance, what she might want from him at her son's wedding, some legal business. No, this is something tender, I suspect, something they can treasure now that they are old. I will not ask. I do not dare to ask.

I am, I have to say, an urban animal. I have not strayed this far from town before, except by boat or plane and only then to end up in another town, where, given that I speak some English and a little French, it is not hard to feel at ease. But here, among the trees, I find not quite a hostile world but an unaccommodating one, unshaped to suit my needs or sensibilities, unsuitable, indeed, for highly polished shoes like mine (and Joseph's, come to that). Already they are soiled. I look back with longing at my elders and see them already hunched forward in conversation over the picnic table, not caring that the green oily mold on its surface and on the benches has already stained their sleeves and would have given them both a slimy derrière if we had not spread out some of Joseph's hamper napkins to sit on. She swings her feet clear of the ground. She does her best not to make contact with the debris or the earth. He is holding up his hands, palms out, surrendering or maybe making an apology. And then, as if acting on a hidden sign, they both stretch out at once to touch the coffer with their fingertips.

My involuntary expedition to the forest is not entirely without purpose. I must pass water. We are all animals where bowels and bladders are concerned. The ground gives way on me alarmingly and cracks beneath my feet as I step into the undergrowth. I do not trust my feet or shoes. I cannot say that it is hard to reach my chosen tree, but it is cumbersome and tricky. The forest seems to want to seize me by my ankles. The smells that are released by every step I take are venomous. The sounds I hear are unfamiliar. I must admit to feeling fearful—how rational is that?—and cannot wait to urinate and then blunder back as quickly as I can to open ground.

My tree trunk is more than wide enough to conceal me from my companions—can I call them friends?—and hide them from me as well. I cannot help but be reminded of a Busi song: "You can't be seen, you always say / But you are not invisible / Though out of sight / You're in my light / And on display / Through every loving moment / Of my day." I have a sense that I am being watched and have to check before I open up my fly. Mrs. Pencillon and Mr. Busi are still in happy conversation, though they have both sat back from Alicia's coffer and now seem to be laughing. And Lex is crashing about somewhere far enough away. No, what I fear are creatures watching me. I almost feel the weight of them across my back. I can anticipate their claws and teeth. Oh, how I'd rather be inside the bathroom of a house with a bolted door at my back and curtains on the outside world than on show like this, a urinating beast, and unprotected from the world. So I make haste. I brace myself with a single arm against the body of a tree I can't identify or name and watch the line of timber ants marching in single file through the bark's canyons and ravines. My water interrupts their climb. It washes some of them away as well as coaxing from the bark a sweet and unexpected smell akin to licorice.

Even when I've finished urinating and my trousers are secured, I am still oddly fearful of attack, more fearful than I've ever been in town. The tales I've heard from Mr. Busi in recent months about that cruel assault on him in the Mendicant Gardens have not made me less secure in streets and alleyways or even on the promenade at night. I walk there often, unperturbed. I don't imagine being bitten or scratched or kicked or robbed, either by man or beast. The bosk has gone, the streets are cleared, there's nothing wild for me to fear. But out here in the shadows of the forest, with its unceasing commentary of sounds, the dangers seem to press upon me, as if the air itself is mothy with indifference. I'm almost glad to hear a human voice. It's Lex. She's calling me. It's time, she says. It's time for anniversaries and funerals, the major ceremonies of life that none of us avoid. I find her standing thigh-deep in the undergrowth, excited by the prospects of some rites and with Mr. Busi's Persian bells draped across her arms like a string of rosaries.

My landlord has granted Lex permission to organize the scattering. While I've been urinating in the woods, she has found some implement—a piece of jagged metal from a dismantled truck or car—with which to scoop out a knee-deep hole in the softer ground where the autumns have provided layers of leaf mold. Already she has lined the hole with ferns and flowers and placed the open produce box at its center, ready for . . . whatever she has planned. The medals, the villa's ancient key, the Venetian *campanello* seem powerful and meaningful now that they are out of town and out of context. They're dislocated and useless here, and symbolic therefore. They are the medals, keys, and bells of life, our thresholds and our vanities, our fast-expiring time.

Now Lex has found a tree to climb. You'd think, to witness it, she clambered in the forest frequently, that in some secret life she was arboreal. She clearly finds it easy to transfer her weight between the branches, using all four limbs in a rotation that seems both natural and risky. She wants to reach the elbow of a high branch that loops directly over the burial hole she's made below. She has to reach far out and stretch, holding on with one hand to a throttle vine, which has wrapped around the trunk but could easily snap, it seems to me. It bends to her weight, and creaks. She holds the Persian bells by her other fingertips and has to swing them several times before she snags them on the nub of a twig.

"Some bird will have them for its nest if you leave them there," I say, the helpful street-lubber who hasn't ever climbed a tree that high or even wanted to.

So she has to free them from the twig and try again, taking even greater risks to tie them round the branch with their own chain, so that no animal or bird can claim them as a trophy without the help of fingers or the aid of tools. At last, she's satisfied. She draws back to the trunk and, using only her upper limbs, lowers herself to the ground. The Persian bells are swinging under their own weight and tinkling in the summer breeze. "That's it," she says, cleaning her hands on her skirts. "Let's start."

"I'll fetch them, shall I?"

"No," she says, "we have to summon them by bell."

She takes the heavy—and expensive—*campanello* out of the produce box and hits it firmly, though a little tonelessly, with the piece of metal she has used to dig the hole. I have to hold it by its chain so that she can strike it for a second time and find a truer, louder, clearer note. Then I have to go across to offer my arm to Mrs. Pencillon and help her to take the short walk between the picnic bay and where her sister's ashes will be spread. As we draw near, with Mr. Busi close behind, Lex intones the Latin tag *"Qui me tangit vocem meam audi,"* "Whoever strikes me, hears my voice." It will be our pagan liturgy today. She will not stop reciting it or hitting dull notes on the bell until the widow and the widower have unsealed the coffer, dipped their fingers several times into Alicia's remains, and let them float through broken sunlight to the ground. Now Lex proclaims a prayer she has prepared, a string of *may she*s, *let there*s, and *forever*s. It's no more vacuous than those you hear in crematoria and churches, and at least it mentions all of us by name including—several times—Alicia. "Amen," she cannot stop herself from saying when she's done and cannot help but look shamefaced.

In turn, with Mr. Busi last, we throw handfuls of leaf mold into the hole that Lex has prepared, until the produce box, together with the medals and the *campanello*, have been entirely covered, first with vegetation, then with earth. Above us, Mr. Busi's wife is standing at the larder door. We hear its timber creak and then we hear the Persian bells, betraying her a final time. They play the song that still has not discovered words.

"Like a sewer," Mr. Busi says, and meets Lex's and Mrs. Pencillon's raised eyebrows with his calmest smile. "Yes, like a sewer," he repeats. "Long, deep, and wide."

The sun is sinking into the forest already, and at our backs we hear our driver, Albert, and his car arrive in the clearings. He switches off his engine but leaves his headlamps on, to let us know that he is there and ready to return us to the town. Mr. Busi is dry-eyed, unlike his sister-in-law, but I can tell how moved he is and satisfied. I find the courage, seeing he is so close to me, to reach across and rest a hand on his shoulder, like a son. Then Mrs. Pencillon does the same, at his other shoulder, like a sister, like a friend. He has epaulettes of hands to take the place of all those medals he has parted with.

"There's one more thing," he says at last. At his request, Lex and I bring the hamper over from the picnic bench and we spread the foods we have not managed to dispatch ourselves across the swollen patch of ground where we have interred the produce box and on which his wife's ashes have been scattered. Above us, bells maintain the melody.

Joseph might have overcatered for the human four of us, but nobody can overcater for the hunger in the Park. There are dainty sandwiches and cheese, slices of cold meats and salmon, the contents of six costly jars, hardly touched by us, pâté, olives, and foie gras. And of course there are the pastries and the cakes, the fancy breads and slices. We go back to the car, where it is safe, and—wondering, just wondering, what we will witness at the forest edge—we wait there in its headlamp beams for creatures to appear and dine.

ACKNOWLEDGMENTS

I am indebted to *Mister Al, the Singer and the Songs: A Personal Memoir* by Richard Vince, *Celui qui doit vivre* by Victor Hugo, the *Indices* archive kept by the University of Texas at Austin, the Dobie Paisano Ranch, also in Austin (where this volume was completed), and the Estate of Mrs. Marianne Pencillon.

A Note About the Author

Jim Crace is the author of eleven previous novels. His most recent, *Harvest,* was short-listed for the Man Booker Prize and won the International Dublin Literary Award and the James Tait Black Memorial Prize. In 2000, *Being Dead* won the U.S. National Book Critics Circle Award for Fiction, and in 1997, *Quarantine* was named the Whitbread Novel of the Year and was short-listed for the Booker Prize. Jim Crace has also received the Whitbread First Novel Prize, the E. M. Forster Award, and the Guardian Fiction Prize. He lives in Worcestershire, England.

A Note About the Type

Pierre Simon Fournier *le jeune* (1712–1768), who designed the type used in this book, was both an originator and a collector of types. His services to the art of printing were his design of letters, his creation of ornaments and initials, and his standardization of type sizes. His types are old style in character and sharply cut. In 1764 and 1766 he published his *Manuel typographique,* a treatise on the history of French types and printing, on typefounding in all its details, and on what many consider his most important contribution to typography—the measurement of type by the point system.